WANTED

FUGITIVE MARINES | BOOK 2

DAVID RYKER
DOUGLAS SCOTT

RYKER'S ROGUES

PROLOGUE

He'd been known as Dr. Toomey for so long that even he had actually come to think of himself by that name, even though it didn't remotely resemble the one he'd been given at birth. Not that it mattered—a rose by any other name would smell as sweet, according to the Bard. Toomey, of course, didn't put any stock in Shakespeare himself, or the works of any poet, for that matter. He preferred reading abstracts and studies by authors with long strings of letters after their names. As far as he was concerned, that was where the future lay.

At the moment, he was reading one of his own equations on the holographic white board that took up the east wall of his lab. The board was connected via wi-fi to a series of sensors currently monitoring an interface between a lump of nanite clay and a similar lump of lab-grown flesh on the table behind him. The flesh was not responding the way he wanted it to when the clay changed form, and it was frustrating him.

Dr. Toomey did *not* like being frustrated.

He turned to the table and leaned closer to the subject of his experiment. As he did, the sensors picked up his features and broadcast them into the display. He saw himself—gaunt face, bald pate, serious eyes behind serious electronic spectacles—floating in three dimensions and looking back at him. He wasn't amused. Dr. Toomey couldn't remember the last time he'd been amused.

"Doctor," said a voice over the commlink.

He saw his 3D reflection frown back at him. "Do you know the correct frequency the nanites' amplitude must be aligned to in order to not impede the electrical signals of the nerves of the pseudo-flesh, Mr. White?" he asked.

"Uh, no, sir," said the voice.

"Then why are you interrupting me?"

"You have an important call, sir."

"No, I do not. Take a message."

"Uh, sir, the call is encrypted."

Toomey sighed. An encrypted call meant only one thing. He gave his experiment one final, longing look and strode across the lab to the small room that housed his personal encrypted commlink. The door slid open in front of him, then slid shut behind him, activating a light in the ceiling. He placed a palm on the ID scanner and a green light flashed.

The upper half of Oscar Bloom's body appeared in a floating sphere in front of him. Bloom was at his home office desk. A crystal tumbler three-quarters full of amber liquid sat by his left hand.

"What is it, Oscar? I'm quite busy."

"You're always 'quite busy,' Toomey," said Bloom, a man in late middle age with silver hair and the refined good looks that came with generations of selective breeding. "And I always have to remind you that it's my money that keeps you 'quite busy.'"

Ah, how I enjoy playing petty games with the people who hold the world's purse strings. "Of course, Oscar, how rude of me. What can I do for you?"

"I need you to get a private ship ready and send some supplies out to Oberon One."

The prison station orbiting Oberon where Bloom's prodigal daughter worked? What fresh nonsense was this? Toomey managed to keep himself from simply flipping off the commlink and going back to work, but it was an effort.

"May I ask why?"

Bloom scowled. "It's a long story. All you need to know is that this is your top priority until it's completed."

"It always is, Oscar," Toomey said with a smile that had all the charm of a dead eel.

"You know, Toomey, one of these days, I'm going to smack the smartass right out of you."

"Yes, I'm sure, but that day isn't today. Flash me the details. I'll begin immediately."

"You need to talk with the warden on Oberon One. Farrell's his name. Good guy, understands discretion."

"One would hope," Toomey said drily. "It *is* the nature of everything I do, after all."

Bloom glared at him and downed his glass of scotch at a gulp.

"Just fucking do it," he growled. "Or so help me God, you'll be the one who ends up on the receiving end of the bullshit you people do."

The image disappeared as the words "transmission ended" appeared on the holographic screen, which flicked off a moment later.

Toomey grinned, less creepily this time because he actually felt it.

Yes, he thought. *And then you'll just go to the local recruiting agent and have them find the next smartest man in the world. Then you can put him to work running your personal shadow intelligence and black operations network. How hard could it be?*

He knew he had Bloom over a barrel; just one of many supposedly powerful people he had over a barrel. But because he relied on those people for money and resources, every once in awhile he had to jump through a hoop or two. And that was fine.

He called up the file on Oberon One: a station in orbit around the second largest of the moons of Uranus, built by SkyLode, a mining company in which Oscar Bloom was a major investor. SkyLode had contracted with the new Trilateral Government to house some of the worst criminals on Earth and put them to work mining the surface of the moon for palladium, which was invaluable in fueling the fusion reactors that powered the world. It was a leading-edge example of what were being called "cooperative agreements" these days. Essentially, government services being conducted by private corporations for a profit. In the case of Oberon One, profit came in the form of government grants, a slave labor force of inmates, and, of course, the spoils of the mining operation. SkyLode, for all intents and purposes, owned the moon.

Toomey entered the code for the station's commlink. He noted with mild interest that the quantum teleportation technology on its end rivalled his own. It would make for clear, instantaneous transmissions, at least.

About a minute later, another projection of a silver-haired middle-aged man appeared in front of him. This one was taller than Bloom, and his eyes were... *off* somehow.

"Warden Farrell?" he asked.

"That's me!" the man answered jovially. "And you're the fellow that Mr. Bloom told me would get in touch, I assume?"

"Yes, you can call me Doctor. How can I be of assistance?"

Farrell adopted an abashed look that Toomey instantly saw through. Whatever was going on, this man knew more than he was saying, which Toomey found intriguing.

"Well, Doctor, it's really kind of embarrassing. We've had a bit of a riot on the station."

Toomey arched an eyebrow. "A riot? In space? What, exactly, did the inmates think would be the endgame of that?"

Farrell shrugged. "Who can fathom the mind of a criminal? In any case, we lost a lot of supplies that need replacing, and Mr. Bloom assured me that you could take care of that."

"Indeed. What do you need?"

Farrell manipulated the panel on the portable computer he wore around his wrist and a message flashed on the wall of the commlink room. It was a list of items.

Items that instantly intrigued Dr. Toomey.

"Pardon my curiosity, Warden, but may I ask what use a mining station-slash-prison has for such supplies? You're asking for large amounts of raw materials and electronic components, and yet I don't see any request for palladium. Your reactor still runs on it, yes?"

The warden's eyes widened for just an instant. "Ah, of course. Please add palladium to the list."

"You didn't answer my question. This is a list of items that I might requisition for my own electronic engineering laboratory. Things hardly of use to either inmates or miners."

Farrell gazed at him with those strange eyes for several seconds, giving Toomey time to analyze the man's facial microexpressions. The warden was lying—obviously—but he was also amused. This was fun to him, whatever *this* was. Curious.

"Doctor," he said finally. "Can you keep a secret?"

With great effort, Toomey kept himself from rolling his eyes. He didn't want to scare off his new playmate.

"Yes, Warden Farrell, I can keep a secret. I don't know what Mr. Bloom may have told you about me, but secrecy is a hallmark of the work I do for him."

"I have no doubt." Farrell leaned forward and lowered his voice. "I meant can you keep a secret from Mr. Bloom?"

Now Toomey had to stop himself from grinning. What had started out as a tedious chore was quickly becoming very interesting, indeed.

"I have kept many secrets from many people in my time," he said. "Including Mr. Bloom. I would be happy to extend my discretion to you as well in this matter."

Farrell's smile was wide. His eyes were unreadable, however, which intrigued Toomey even more.

"Well, Doctor, I confess that we've been doing a little more than just mining and rehabilitating criminals here on Oberon One. We discovered something in the moon that's been quite intriguing."

Toomey's eyes narrowed. There were no true scientists on board the station, only technicians trained in maintaining the systems that operated it.

Now, now, he admonished himself. *Remember your own humble beginnings*. He knew better than anyone that great minds weren't exclusive to the halls of academia. Genius simply needed a catalyst to be sparked into life.

Farrell's eyes were practically sparkling now. "Our people have been able to come up with some pretty interesting ideas as a result of this discovery." He lowered his voice again. "Can I shoot you some schematics and technical abstracts? A few of our scans? Encrypted, of course."

"Of course." A few moments later, the data was being projected from Toomey's wristband.

Whatever the doctor had been expecting to see, it wasn't this. His eyes were wider than they'd been in many years, and Dr. Toomey had seen a great many things during his time on Earth that would have left ordinary people speechless had they been privy to them.

"What in the name of...?" he breathed.

"I thought you might be intrigued." Farrell grinned. "Remember, Doctor, you said you could keep a secret. And this one is a real doozy. Now, if you don't mind, I'm going to hand you over to my right-hand man. You'll be dealing with him directly from now on. He's the one who's really plugged into what's happening here on Oberon One.

"His name is Butch Kergan."

1

The fugitives of Oberon had been in space for eighteen days by then, and it was starting to take its toll on them. They were, of course, used to close quarters, having spent between six months and two years on a prison station orbiting a moon of Uranus, but the constant zero-gravity was new.

"Cannae imagine what it's gonna be like when my fat arse is weighin' me down again," said Percival Maggott as he floated through the cargo hold. He was nearly as wide as he was tall, and his muscle-to-fat ratio meant he tipped the scales at a number that would make most people gasp in horror.

"Just try not to be around me when it happens," said Geordie Bishop. His wiry frame was strong, but even he wouldn't have a hope of hefting Maggott's bulk off him. "I don't want people at my funeral asking 'How'd he croak?' and Ellie having to answer, 'Well, he was crushed by a human grizzly from Scotland.'"

Maggott frowned. "Ye dinnae need to worry about wee Ellie," he said. "I'll have her plenty busy."

"All right, stow it, you two," warned Napoleon Quinn, their former Marine commander and current fellow fugitive. "Dev, what's our status?"'

"Just adjusting course now," came Dev Schuster's voice on their helmet headsets from his place at the pilot's controls on the ship's bridge, one level up. "Last asteroid in the field is officially behind us, which means we pass the orbit of Mars and then we see our pretty little blue home planet after that. Just over fifty hours from now."

"A shame our trajectory won't take us past Mars," Bishop sighed. "I hear it's lovely this time of year."

"It wouldn't be if we passed by," said Schuster. "At the speed we're travelling, we'd probably wreak havoc on the gravity if we came within a million kilometers."

"Still cain't wrap m'head 'round that," said Ulysses in his East Texas drawl. He looked different these days, now that a thick coat of stubble had grown in over his previously shaved head and eyebrows. And, of course, they all had three weeks' growth of beard. "Took us over three months to get from Earth to Oberon, and it'll be less'n one goin' back."

"It's weird, all right," said Quinn. Then again, what wasn't weird these days?

"How 'bout you, Doc? How long d'your trip take?"

Chelsea Bloom sighed. "For the last time, Ulysses, I'm not actually a doctor. Call me Chelsea."

"I'm a hardened criminal, Doc. I ain't callin' nobody *Chelsea*."

"Fine," she said, shaking her head. "I was in transit for nine weeks, but the private ship I came on was quite a bit faster than your Corrections Department transport, which was one of the first-generation ships. Not much newer than the Raft we're on right now."

"Excuse me," said Bishop, raising a finger. "I'll thank you to call her by her official designation, if you don't mind."

She rolled her eyes. "Fine, the United Free Territories Spaceship FUBAR. Happy?"

"Got a certain ring to it, dunnit?" Maggott grinned.

"That was true before the upgrade," said Schuster as he floated into the cargo bay from the bridge. "But things are a lot different on this ship now."

That was an understatement if ever Quinn had heard one. The

FUBAR had started life as a multi-purpose military ship for the UFT faction in the Trilateral War, then had been seconded to Oberon One for mining purposes, where it had undergone a radical upgrade under the guiding hand of technician Kevin Sloane, who was under the influence of a hive mind parasite with access to knowledge that was far beyond that of humans.

After Quinn and his companions had broken out of Oberon One, FUBAR had carried them from Uranus to where they were now, passing Mars on their way to Earth. Food, oxygen and fuel had all held, and he was beginning to hold out hope that they might just make it home.

Of course, once they got there, they'd still have to convince the world's leaders to listen to a bunch of fugitives who'd escaped during a riot they started, and who wanted them to believe that there was an interstellar armada headed for Earth, controlled by a species of sentient thoughts that wanted to take over the minds of every person on the planet.

But there would be time for that later. He found it easier to retain some semblance of sanity if he took things one step at a time.

"Speaking of upgrades," said Quinn. "I don't suppose you've found any artificial gravity generators in your memories from Sloane, have you?"

"Sorry, sir. That's not really how my communication with the Sloane part of my brain works. To be honest, I'm not entirely sure of that myself. But I do know that we can't generate gravity in FUBAR. It takes too much energy, even if we had the tech."

"How did people do it in the old days?" Bishop was doing a barrel roll in mid-air. "I mean, back in the early decades of the 21st century, some astronauts would be in the International Space Station for a year or more."

"Those were the days," said Chelsea. "Remember when the world actually got along well enough to cooperate on things like the ISS? They don't agree on much anymore, even after the war was settled."

"They agree that people in the Towers need t'keep gettin' richer," Ulysses muttered.

"They *always* seem ta agree on that," said Maggott. "Foony thing, aye?"

"Speaking of rich people," said Quinn, "I think it's time to get in touch with your father, Chelsea. If we're going to have a hope in hell of not getting locked up the second we come within scanning range of Earth, we'll need his help."

Chelsea bit her lip behind her polycarbonate faceplate. In the eighteen days they'd been locked up together in this ship, Quinn had learned a lot about her character and quirks. And he had to stop himself from dwelling on how much he liked what he was learning. He and his Jarheads would be lucky to survive the week, let alone stay out of prison if and when they made it back to Earth. And even if, by some blue-eyed miracle, they were able to accomplish their mission, there was an alien armada looming on the horizon.

"I'm worried," she said. "My father must have talked to Kergan on the station by now, and we can also be sure that Kergan didn't tell him the truth about what happened. Dad probably assumed we'd rendezvous with the supply ship that's en route to the station already. As far as he knows, it's the only way we could have made it home, because the Rafts don't have that kind of range."

"It wouldn't have done Kergan any good to tell him the truth," said Quinn. "He probably told your father that you and the rest of us would hijack the supply ship and take it back to Earth."

Schuster nodded. "Which means they think we're going to be a lot later than we actually are. The question is, what is Kergan thinking right now? He couldn't tell Chelsea's father what's really going on without raising a bunch of questions about FUBAR's upgraded technology. Questions that Kergan doesn't want to answer."

"Kergan's a wily sumbitch," said Ulysses. "I bet he's just lyin' in wait for that supply ship. Once it shows up, he'll scavenge every piece o' tech off'n it and use it fer his wormhole generator."

"I agree," said Chelsea. "I think we run too big a risk if we get in touch with my father. We've taken our chances so far and come out okay."

Quinn thought about that. They were playing a game of chess

here without being able to see all the pieces on the board. How much had Kergan told Bloom? Could they possibly make it to Earth undetected and start the next phase of their mission without any more trouble than it would already be? Could their luck really be holding?

The answer, of course, was no.

2

The first blast was hard enough to spin FUBAR a full 360 degrees, and was almost enough to make Quinn shit his environment suit. It was a good thing he didn't, because nearly three weeks of constant use had left it smelling ripe enough already. Now within sight of the pale blue marble that was Earth, Quinn had begun to hope they might just make it out of this after all – and almost as importantly, make it to a shower. That should have been his first warning. For the past two years, hell the five before that, very little had gone to plan.

"Where the hell did that come from?" he barked.

It was two days later and the cargo hold was chaos: none of them had bothered to strap themselves in, so they were literally bouncing off the walls. Maggott slammed into the hold's wall hard enough to dent the back plate of his suit and knock the wind out of him.

"Bogeys!" Schuster cried from the bridge. "They just appeared out of nowhere! There was nothing on the scanners until the shot!"

Quinn grabbed the rungs on the wall and pulled himself toward the hatch that led to the bridge while the others made for the jump seats so they could lock themselves in place. Once on the bridge,

Quinn could see the big main screen that showed them everything the ship's cameras were picking up.

There were no fewer than five ships on their tail, all military-grade Rafts. But they looked sleeker, somehow, and they were flying a lot more smoothly than the pigs the Jarheads had used as transports in the war.

"Those things have clearly gone through some upgrades of their own," he said, staring at the screen.

"I've got the shields up, sir," said Schuster. "But I don't know if we need them. That blast wasn't full-on plasma, it was some kind of concussive force. If they're trying to blow us out of the sky, they're using the wrong weapon."

"Maybe they're *not* trying to blow us out of the sky. How did the ship not detect them before now?"

"I don't know. They should have picked up anything in orbit as soon as we got inside the moon's orbit. They must have stealth tech that makes them invisible to sensors. The only way they can be tracked is with the naked eye."

"I heard talk about experiments in that vein during the war, but I didn't know they were anywhere near development."

Quinn looked closely at the camera feeds as the incoming ships began to flank them. Below them was the big blue marble of Earth. He would have been sentimental about their return home if they weren't under fire.

"I don't see any military insignias," he pointed out.

"With upgrades like that, they're almost certainly private. Which probably means one thing, sir."

He nodded. "Kergan told Oscar Bloom we were coming."

Chelsea's voice came over the headset: "I can still try getting in touch with him, have him call off his dogs!"

"Not yet," said Quinn. "We'll ride this out. There hasn't been a follow-up shot yet, and that last one was just meant to let us know they're there."

"Attention unidentified vessel!" A voice broke into their frequency and blared through their headsets. "Stand down and join formation!

We will escort you to the surface, where you will be taken into custody!"

"Jarheads, total radio silence," Quinn muttered, then, more loudly: "This is UFT Marine Cap—uh, I mean Sergeant—shit. This is Napoleon Quinn. Who the hell are you?"

"I'm the guy who has five Destroyer-class Fortresses following you and your band of fugitives," said the voice. "And that little slap on the ass was just a taste of what you're going to get if you don't fall into formation RFN!"

"RFN?" Chelsea whispered.

"Right fucking now," Quinn whispered back. He knew that old-fashioned texting language was the hallmark of mercenaries with no formal military background. It traced all the way back to the oil skirmishes of the early 2030s, when private armies first began to get traction.

He held up four fingers to Schuster, who responded by changing the frequency of his headset. "Orders, sir?"

"How firm is your grasp of FUBAR's weapons systems?"

"Firm enough. Not to argue, sir, but wouldn't it make more sense to just let them force us down and take us in rather than risk a fight?"

Quinn looked up at the screen in front of them, divided to show a 360-degree view of the ship. The Fortresses were already beginning to take formation around them, but it was tighter than it should be. And something about the voice over the radio was raising his hackles.

"Unidentified vessel, what is your ship's data transmission signature?" the voice said in Quinn's right ear. He had two frequencies going at once and it was a bit distracting. "We'll flash you an unlocking sequence that will allow us to pilot your ship by remote."

Quinn hit a control on his wrist to switch his microphone. "Stand by." To Schuster, he said: "You're allowed to argue with me, Dev. You all are. I'm not your commander anymore."

"You'll be my commander for two weeks after I'm dead, sir. I was just curious what your reasoning was."

Quinn frowned. "You said to let them take us in. Here's the thing: I'm pretty sure that the only one who'll get taken in is

Chelsea. The rest of us will get taken *out*, if you get my meaning. And we don't even know where we're going, just that we have to find Major Zheng. We'll probably end up surrendering eventually just to get on the ground, but I hate going into any situation without a plan."

Schuster nodded. He settled back into the pilot's seat and hit the control that switched them from auto to manual. The console split in half and a joystick rose from the floor and locked into position between his knees.

"Ready to play," he said. "Just the plasma cannons, as far as I know, and the shields, but that should be enough to buy you some time."

Quinn patted his shoulder. "You're a true mensch, Sergeant." Into the other channel, he said: "Stand by. We're determining the frequency."

"Hurry the hell up!" came the reply.

"Definitely not military," Quinn said over their own radio. "Which means I don't care what happens to them. Do whatever you want, Dev."

Schuster grinned. "Sir, yes *sir!*"

There was an opening to their starboard side and Schuster took it, diving through the hole and breaking formation.

"What the fuck are you doing?!" the voice hollered, but Quinn wasn't listening. He tethered himself to the bridge wall to keep from being tossed around by FUBAR's maneuvering.

"All right, Jarheads, radio silence lifted," he said. "Here's the situation: these guys are here for Chelsea, and the rest of us are collateral damage. That means they won't blast us out of the sky, but we need to have a plan in place for when we get on the ground. I'm sure we can escape from whoever's waiting to meet us down there, but we need to find Zheng first."

"I can call Ellie," said Bishop. "It's a gamble, but I think we need to take it and pray she found the Major."

"Get on it," said Quinn. "Chelsea, when we get on the ground, we'll hand you over first. I'll do everything I can to make sure you're safe before we attempt our escape, but I'm afraid I can't guarantee anything."

The ship banked to the right and Quinn grabbed on the rung next to him for extra support. On the monitor, the Fortresses were scrambling to follow. He heard soft shouts coming through on the second frequency, barely audible now that he'd turned the volume down.

"What are you talking about, Quinn?" Chelsea said in his ear.

"Under other circumstances, your safety would be our top priority, but this is—well, unique. I mean, we're talking about the end of the world here. The mission has to come first."

"I'm *on* the mission, you jackass! I'm not going with them!"

"Holy shit," Maggott breathed. "She just called th' captain a jackass."

"He's not *my* captain!" she fumed.

"I'm not anybody's captain!" Quinn snapped. "All right, I get it, you're with us. I just didn't want to speak for you."

She scoffed. "Jesus, I came *this* far with you clowns! You think I'm going to bail now?"

Quinn felt a bizarre swell of pride. Chelsea wasn't one of his men, but she was a member of the team now. The fact that she was willing to follow him made him feel like maybe, just maybe, he could stop an alien invasion.

"Yeah, don't y'all go askin' what *I'm* gonna do," Ulysses grumbled. "Assholes."

"We know *you're* in," Quinn said with a chuckle. "You're like us, you got no choice."

The ship dropped suddenly and Quinn went shooting upward, knocking his helmet against the roof of the bridge.

"Sorry, sir!" Schuster yelped. "Took another shot from above! They're not too happy about this!"

"Give 'em a taste of their own medicine," Quinn growled. He could already feel a knot forming on the top of his skull.

"Oorah!" Schuster pulled FUBAR up into a climb, and the monitor showed the underbelly of one of the Fortresses. He let go with the plasma cannon on their nose, and Quinn watched as tiny explosions rocked the ship.

"All right, then," he said. "We're all in. When these bastards take us down, we come out firing. Agreed?"

"Uh, sir," said Maggott. "We got no weapons on board." In his Scottish brogue, it came out as *weepuns*.

Quinn sighed. "Shit. I forgot about that. I guess we'll improvise. We always do."

Chelsea surprised him by giggling. "How the hell did you people stay alive during five years of war?"

Quinn snorted a chuckle himself. "Somebody's watching over for us, except our guardian angel is a sadistic prick."

"Vegas!" Bishop hooted over the headset.

"I don't know if we can get leave for a vacation right now, Geordie."

"Zheng is in Vegas! Ellie found him, God bless her, she started hitchhiking south right after my last call to her from Oberon One. She's almost there now."

"Give that girl a field commission!" Quinn crowed. "Vegas! We have a destination!"

"Vegas, baby!" Ulysses sounded even more excited than Quinn felt. "That's on the edge o' Southern Saints territory. We get there, I can get us whatever we need."

"Better and better," said Quinn. "The only one who shit on this parade was you, Maggott. Why'd you have to point out we don't have any weapons?"

"I *am* a weapon," Maggott said quietly. "I can sacrifice m'self so that you c'n get away."

And suddenly the jovial mood was gone. Quinn knew the big man meant what he said, and worse, it was actually a decent plan. Desperate times, desperate measures. But Napoleon Quinn had made a silent vow to his men when they joined him on that prison transport to Oberon One two years earlier: he would do everything in his power to repay their loyalty, and sending one of them to their death would be breaking that vow.

"Dev, is there anything on FUBAR that might be able to get us away from these bastards?"

"There might be, sir, but if there is, I haven't found it yet."

"And you can't just, like, do a web search in your head?"

"Little busy right now, sir," he said with mild petulance.

Quinn felt abashed. "You're right, sorry. Just spitballing."

"It's a good idea, I just need the time to try it. And unfortunately, none of you can take over flying the ship."

I really don't want to do this, Quinn thought grimly. But what choice was there?

"How long will it take to get to the surface if we surrender?" he asked.

Schuster looked back over his shoulder at him. "Probably twenty minutes. Why?"

"Is that long enough to do what you need to do?"

"I suppose it'll have to be."

"All right, then. Good luck."

"Hey," said Chelsea. "Are you saying what I think you're saying?"

Quinn didn't answer her. Instead, he opened his microphone to the secondary frequency and turned up the volume.

"—blow you out of the fucking sky—"

"Shut up," said Quinn. "Our data transmission signature is Foxtrot Uniform Charlie Kilo—"

"You want another blast up your tailpipe, smartass?"

Quinn grinned. Sometimes it was the little things that meant the most, and these days, he would take all the little things he could get.

"All right, all right." He gave the pilot the proper signature. "We'll come quietly."

"You fucking well better," came the reply.

Schuster worked the controls for a few seconds and FUBAR's attitude shifted. On the screens, the other ships were aligning around them.

"That's it," said Quinn. "We've got twenty minutes. It's up to you, Dev."

Schuster sighed. "Why can't anything ever be easy?"

3

Five minutes later, Dev Schuster would have been pulling his hair if his head wasn't encased in the helmet of his environment suit.

"Not working?" Quinn asked.

"It's hard to explain, sir. The thoughts are there, I just can't get to them. It's like they're locked in boxes made of opaque glass. I can see their outline, but no details. I know FUBAR is capable of more, I just don't know *what*, exactly."

Quinn sighed. "Well, it was worth a shot."

The Earth glowed blue on the monitor in front of them, and Quinn turned to look out the porthole at the real thing. He'd seen it from space many times during the war, and once while being transported to prison, but now it took on a whole new significance. It was as if it were made of glass now, so incredibly fragile. Its fate rested on their shoulders, and he was beginning to feel that weight.

"If only everyone could see her from up here," he said softly.

"Sir?"

"Just woolgathering. Maybe if people could look at the Earth as a whole instead of their own little piece of it, we wouldn't have so many wars."

"Sir, that's it!"

Quinn blinked. "What's it?"

"I need radio silence," said Schuster, ignoring him.

"You heard him," said Quinn.

Schuster unlocked the harness that had been keeping him in the pilot's seat and floated freely into the center of the bridge. Quinn, still tethered to the wall, watched but kept his questions to himself. As he did, Schuster bent himself into a position where his legs were wrapped around each other and his spine was straight. It couldn't have been easy in his environmental suit, but he managed it. Finally, he dropped his elbows to his knees and clasped his thumbs to his middle fingers.

"Here goes nothing," Schuster muttered. After that, all Quinn heard from him was deep breathing.

~

"How long have I been here?"

The space around him was all colors and no colors at the same time, and he was worried that he was wasting time by staring at it. But it was just so fascinating...

"Time is of no consequence," said a voice.

A presence formed in Schuster's field of vision, slowly solidifying into a ball of glowing light. It felt warm, somehow, even though he was pretty sure he wasn't actually feeling anything with his skin. He was feeling it with his mind.

"Where am I?" he asked. "Who are you?"

"You're in the astral plane. I think you know who I am."

Whoa. It had actually worked. Dev Schuster had felt a sudden inspiration when Quinn had mentioned looking at the whole instead of the pieces, and had attempted to enter a meditative state to help him change his perspective.

"Don't break your arm patting yourself on the back," said his new companion. "I was the one who brought you here."

"Are you really Sloane?" Schuster was wary. The real Kevin Sloane had

been taken over by an alien intelligence on Oberon One, but in the end, the two seemed to have merged into a single entity. Part of that entity had somehow entered Schuster's mind when Sloane was killed.

"I've been attempting contact for weeks in your dimension," said the egg. "You have been resisting."

"Not resisting, exactly. More like I didn't know what you were trying to do."

"You needed to let go of your conscious focus on your corporeal dimension. Thought is the basis of reality."

"Yeah, well, I didn't take Metaphysics 101 in school, all right? We're in a jam right now and I don't have time to go over this stuff."

"Time is of—"

"Shut up and listen. We can chat about what the hell all this *is between us later, and believe me, I want to know just how worried I should be about having you in my brain. But for right now, I need to know everything the Raft can do."*

The egg paused, and for a moment, Schuster was worried he had offended it. How does one offend an egg?

Then he felt a wave that was as powerful as a physical tsunami smash into him and send him flying.

"Dev!"

"Huh?"

Quinn unhooked himself and floated over to Schuster, taking him by the shoulders. "You gasped really loud. What's the matter?"

"Long story. Push me back to the pilot's seat."

Quinn did as he was told and Schuster strapped himself back in.

"You found something?" he asked.

"You could say that. FUBAR's got cloaking tech."

"Cloaking?" Ulysses' voice came over the headset. "Hate to tell ya, dude, but them boys already know where we are. What good is jamming their sensors gonna do?"

"We won't be jamming their sensors." Schuster manipulated the control panel on the side of his console. "I'm going to override their remote system."

"How?" asked Quinn.

"Change our signature. I like the one you gave them before."

"Then what?" asked Bishop. "What's the damn plan?"

"Hail Mary," said Schuster. "Just like always. Stand by."

Quinn felt tense seconds pass as Schuster manipulated the controls and scanned a series of readouts. Whatever came next, he knew they all had to be ready for it.

"Not to bug you, Dev, but a little more info would be appreciated."

"I can't get us to Vegas, but I can get us to San Antonio."

"That's my old stompin' grounds!" Ulysses hooted.

"Why Texas?" asked Quinn.

"We need to come in over the Gulf Coast," said Schuster.

"Why?"

"Because we're going to run out of power really quickly, and we need to be able to do a water landing if need be. On our current trajectory, San Antonio's the biggest major port on the way to Vegas."

"Why're we gonna run outta power?" asked Maggott.

Schuster's hand hovered over the control panel. "Because we're going to use it all up bending light around the ship. When I hit this button, it'll unlock FUBAR from outside control. Once we're free, I'll activate the cloak and we can make a run for the surface."

"Bending light?" Quinn asked, incredulous.

"Yup." Schuster's eyes were locked on his screens. "Get ready."

"What do the rest of us do?" asked Chelsea.

"Prayer couldn't hurt," said Quinn.

"And hold on tight," added Schuster. "We're going to gave a bumpy ride in."

He hit the controls. Three seconds later, a voice came over the radio: "What the hell...?"

"Here we go."

Quinn saw the monitor in front of them go white as Schuster took control of the stick. A moment later, the sensor readout replaced the camera feed, so that they were flying on instruments, and the light inside the bridge cabin dimmed.

"What happened?" he asked, dumbfounded.

"Light is bending around us," said Schuster. "Basically, it means they can't see us. But it's also bending around our cameras, so they're not able to pick up a visual either."

"Where the fuck did they go?" a voice screamed over the radio.

"FUBAR has stealth tech that matches theirs," said Schuster. "So we're masking our heat signature, radio transmissions, anything that can be picked up by their sensors, just like they did to us. But the light bending allows us to fly right next to them without being seen. They look out their porthole or their camera feeds, all they see is empty space where we are."

"Son of a bitch," Quinn breathed.

"But the power level is already dropping to critical." Schuster pointed to a readout that showed a line moving quickly from right to left.

"How the hell—"

Schuster lowered the volume on their escort's tirade. "I'm going to pour it on so that we can get into the atmosphere and flying level as soon as we can. At this altitude, a small change in trajectory will make a big difference."

Quinn nodded. "Good work. What about air traffic once we hit the atmosphere?"

"That's the bumpy part. I'm going to have to weave around ships that can't detect us. That's why I chose San Antonio instead of Yuma where the Gulf of California comes in, even though it's closer to Vegas. The traffic around San Antonio is a fraction of that over Yuma. We'll have a longer way to go on the ground, but we have a better chance of actually *making it* to the ground."

"God bless that big, fat brain of yours, Sergeant."

"Oi! Nobody ever blesses my fat *arse!*" Maggott said with mock indignation.

The sensors showed their heat signature spike as FUBAR hit the Earth's atmosphere. It lasted a few seconds before dropping again. A few seconds after that, Quinn could feel gravity starting to tug at him again, for the first time in almost three weeks.

"You feel it, Dev?"

"Yessir. I'm okay."

The terrain on the sensor readout showed their descent trajectory, then switched to a different view when they leveled out. The map, in digital satellite imagery, revealed that they were coming in hot over the Atlantic, about a thousand kilometers east of the remains of Puerto Rico. The island had been flooded since the mid-2060s, after a string of catastrophic earthquakes that had also pushed back the Gulf Coast from Corpus Christi to San Antonio, and driven the Gulf of California's shoreline north to Yuma.

The power readout seemed to be picking up speed as the bar moved to the left. At the same time, FUBAR's sensors were showing dozens of aircraft in their flight path. Schuster was manipulating the joystick like a pro, which reminded Quinn to strap in to his jump seat before he got smashed into the ceiling again.

"Hold tight," he said.

"Good thing I didn't have any lunch," Ulysses groaned.

"I didn't realize how heavy I really was until just now," said Chelsea. "Who'd have thought the slop on Oberon One would actually make me gain weight?"

Quinn chuckled in spite of himself. Defiant to the end, all of them. The devil would have to wrestle them all through the gates of hell, kicking and screaming.

"Shit!"

Quinn felt his stomach tumble as FUBAR suddenly dropped steeply. Schuster was wrestling with the controls to get them back on course. The computer map said they had reached the outskirts of San Antonio and were no longer over the water. Their altitude was now lower than the average height of a Tower, which meant they'd be encountering the smog bank any second.

"Sorry," he said. "Didn't account for the slipstream around that transport."

"Uh, Dev," said Quinn. "The bar is all the way to the left now."

The horizontal graph had disappeared and was replaced by a flashing red readout.

"Okay," said Schuster. "That little stunt drained what we had left getting us back level. We're on emergency reserve power now."

"Which means?"

Suddenly the cameras kicked in and Quinn could see out the porthole again. Unfortunately, they were in the smog bank, so all he could see was a brown cloud, except for the gleaming needle of a Tower, way off in the distance, glittering in the sunlight of the clear sky above them.

"Which means the cloak just kicked out, for one thing. Also it means we're essentially gliding now. Luckily we're in the smog bank, so traffic is lighter."

"I honestly thought I'd never see Earth again," Bishop said.

"We're going to be seeing it up close and personal really soon if we don't figure out where to land," said Schuster.

"Where we at?" asked Ulysses. He was climbing through the hatch from the cargo area to the bridge.

Schuster checked his readout. "Eastern outskirts."

"Head for Converse."

Quinn turned to him. "Converse? What's that?"

"Converse ain't nothin,' just another slum. It's what's east o' there that's important: Randolph Air Force Base."

"Air Force?" said Maggott. "Ent been an Air Force in forty years, ever since aircraft were integrated inta the other branches."

"Yeah-bob," said Ulysses. "That's why it's abandoned. There's a slum settlement in the buildings, but there's plenty o' empty landin' strip just waitin' for somebody to use it."

Quinn turned back to Schuster. "Sounds like as good a plan as any. What do you think?"

"I think we don't have a choice. We just lost the last of our power, but we're on the trajectory to Randolph. We couldn't turn now if we wanted to."

The smog outside the window lessened as FUBAR emerged through the bottom of the thickest part of the smog bank. The remains of old buildings flew past underneath them for several seconds, until suddenly they were outside the city limits and into what used to be known as suburbs decades ago, which meant fewer tall buildings to worry about crashing into.

"There it is," said Ulysses, pointing at the monitor. "See it?"

Quinn could make out a cluster of buildings in the distance, mostly collapsed. A few were still intact; they all sported red roofs. On either side were clearings covered in khaki-colored scrub which he assumed used to be airstrips.

"On course," said Schuster. "Thank Heaven for small favors."

Then the screen in front of them went blank and the light went out, plunging the bridge into darkness broken only by a narrow stream of light coming in through the porthole.

"Uh-oh."

"Is it dark up there, too?" Chelsea called.

Quinn scowled. "Yup."

"Okay, good. Just wanted to make sure we were all going to die together."

"We're totally dead now," said Schuster. "Even emergency auxiliary is gone."

"What's our airspeed?" asked Quinn.

"Hundred and forty knots. We might survive impact, but we definitely won't be too happy about it."

"Well," said Quinn, looking out the porthole at the rapidly approaching ground. "Here we are again. You know the drill, folks. Honor to serve with you, yadda yadda."

"Back atcha," said Maggott. "Avenge m'death, n'all that."

"Banzai," said Bishop.

Quinn suddenly remembered Senpai Sally's final word before throwing herself in front of a blast meant for him on this same ship, what seemed like eons ago even though it had been less than a month. Again, he felt his emotions rising up into his throat, and he fought them back.

"I got faith even if y'all don't," said Ulysses, dropping a hand on

Schuster's shoulders just as the ship began to buck and shake from the wind shear. They would hit the rapidly rising ground in seconds.

Schuster leaned back in his seat. "Prepare for impact."

An instant later, they were gliding smoothly again.

"What...?" Quinn asked.

Schuster looked around, blinking. "I don't—" Then his face lit up. "Wait a minute! Inertial dampening!"

"Speak English!" Maggott barked.

"The modifications Sloane made! He said something about how the thrusters were designed to redistribute inertia! They must operate independent of the main power supply somehow!"

"I still don't get what's happening!" said Chelsea.

"I saw it when we took the ship down to the surface of Oberon the last time! The thrusters didn't kick up any dust, and Sloane said it was because our downwards momentum was being redistributed outwards. It must be part of an emergency landing system with its own power supply that kicks in automatically!"

They glided in silence for several more seconds before FUBAR's belly finally touched down on the weed-choked ground underneath them. They pitched forward when their momentum was halted by something that had snagged the ship somehow.

They were quiet a few more seconds. Quinn found himself wishing he could pinch through the material of his environment suit to make sure he wasn't dreaming.

"We're not dead," Bishop breathed.

"We're on the ground," said Chelsea. "My God."

Quinn clapped Schuster on the back. "Good work, Sergeant."

"Yes sir," he sighed.

"All right, all right," said Ulysses. "If y'all are done, I wanna open that hatch and breathe some sweet ol' Texas smog. I spent the last two years cooped up in a cell or a ship. I want some goddamn *space* again."

They could all get behind that idea.

4

In an office in a suite in a Tower in San Francisco, a man sat rubbing his eyes with his left hand. If he did so with his right one, he would run the risk of crushing his eyeballs, so he tended to keep it away from the vulnerable parts of his body.

"They didn't disappear," he said, trying to keep his voice even. "You lost them."

The expression of the man in the holographic projection darkened. "I bloody well didn't!" he snapped. "I'm telling you, the ship literally disappeared from the center of the formation! One second it was there, the next it was gone!"

The man listened intently, nodding in sympathy. "Oh, well, now I understand, Albright. So I'll just go ahead and tell my boss that they suddenly broke the laws of physics on you, and there was nothing you could do about it. Is that what you're saying?"

Albright frowned. "Well, not when you put it *that* way."

"There's some other way to put it, is there?"

He watched as Albright's holographic face worked, bunching, mouth opening and closing, brows drawing down, eyes darting around. Finally, he appeared to give up.

"I'll keep looking for them," he said. The bitterness in his voice was palpable. "The trajectory they were on would take them somewhere in southern Nevada, or maybe Utah. Maybe even Arizona."

"That's an awfully big area, Albright. How exactly do you expect to find them if they can disappear on you?"

Albright scowled. "I suppose *you* know where they're going, then?"

The man smiled. "As a matter of fact, I do. Get your team to Las Vegas as soon as possible and wait there for me. I'll join you within forty-eight hours."

"Vegas? How do you know that?"

The man shut off the commlink call without answering. He was tired of Albright questioning his orders. That was the problem with mercenaries: like all contractors, they each thought they were the boss. He'd take a real soldier any day. But then, real soldiers couldn't do what he and his men could do. Not if they wanted to stay out of prison.

He stood from his spot at the sleek, low desk and strode across the rich carpet toward a small door. Outside the office's floor-to-ceiling windows, the sky was cobalt blue under a blazing sun. Just like it was every day at this altitude.

He tapped a panel with his left palm and the door opened on a small room. He closed the door behind him and sat in the room's lone chair, then manipulated the controls for his personal encrypted commlink. Moments later, a disembodied voice told him the doctor was busy.

He sighed. Toomey was always busy.

"Get him *now* or I'll show up on your doorstep."

He checked his chronometer. Thirty-three seconds later, Toomey's gaunt, pale face filled the holosphere in front of him.

"What is it, Agent Zero?" Toomey snipped. "I'm in the middle of something."

"Your men lost the ship. And with it, Bloom's daughter, not to mention Quinn and his men."

Toomey blinked behind his glasses. "How?"

Zero grinned coldly. "It just disappeared. One second it was there, the next it was gone."

"That's unexpected. We'll have to deal with it."

Zero cocked an eyebrow. "*Unexpected?* It's bullshit is what it is. You need to dispose of those clowns. They were obviously outmaneuvered."

"It's not necessarily—ahem—*bullshit*." Toomey looked as if the word was actually physically in his mouth. "It's possible that they were using advanced technology. Are you able to track them another way?"

Advanced technology? Invisibility was beyond anything Zero knew of in the realm of possibility. Even Toomey hadn't come up with anything like it.

"Yes, I know how to find them," he said. "But before I do, I want to know what I'm getting into. What kind of tech might they have?"

"I can't say, but you should assume that they will be able to match you and your team. By which I mean you may need to employ strategy for a change."

"Very funny. In any case, I'm sure they're headed for Vegas."

"How are you sure, if they disappeared?"

"One, their trajectory was taking them to the southwest. Two, Vegas is where Zheng lives."

Toomey was silent for several seconds. "That would be logical, given their historical behavior patterns. Very well, keep me apprised."

"Will do."

"One more thing, Zero."

He rolled his eyes. "What?"

Toomey's tone was stern. "Remember that Chelsea Bloom is precious cargo, as in the most precious cargo you can imagine. Your men are to treat her with the care they would use on a live nuclear weapon. Understood?"

"Understood," he sighed. "Zero out."

He shut off the commlink and left the room. Back in his spacious office, he poured himself a scotch from the bar that matched his sleek, low desk and stared out the window. There were three other

Towers on the horizon beyond his wall of windows, each one identical to his own. They had to be, since they were supposed to be paragons of equality, as each was the headquarters of one of the factions of the Trilateral Government. In reality, they were nowhere near equal, but appearances were important, especially here in the new capital city.

The tower where Zero's office was located was the fourth column, the joint administrative building that housed all the government departments. And some, like his own, that merely *looked* like government departments.

Appearances. Zero, of all people, knew they could also be deceiving. He knocked back the last of his scotch and ambled over to the mirror that stood on the wall above the mini-sink set in the top of the bar. His reflection looked back at him: wide face, hawk nose, bland features, short blond hair.

Then he slid the cuff of his jacket up over his right wrist, and the flesh split along a microscopic seam there, rising to expose a small panel set into his forearm. With his left hand, he manipulated a set of controls and looked back in the mirror.

The flesh of his face suddenly crawled and bunched, flattening in some areas and bending in others, while his bone structure seemed to narrow and his nose lengthened by several millimeters. The process took about ten seconds.

When it was done, it was Napoleon Quinn's face looking back at him.

"Can't wait to see you again, Captain," he said softly. In his reflection, his right eye briefly flashed a glowing red.

5

"Found it."

Bishop emerged from the rear of the ship with a device about the size of a fishing tackle box. He set it on the scrub several meters from where FUBAR had finally come to rest in the middle of a scrub field. If there was anyone around to witness their landing, they hadn't emerged in the fifteen minutes since it had happened.

"Whassat contraption?" asked Ulysses, pointing at the box.

"Holographic camouflage," said Quinn as he knelt to manipulate the controls. "Standard issue on most military aircraft. It scans the surrounding area and projects a real-time broadcast in 3D around the ship. Runs on a Prometheus battery, so it should be good for several days."

"That ain't gonna fool anyone around here."

"I don't care about scavengers; they won't be able to get in. We just need to make sure she isn't detected from the air. It won't be long before whoever was after us starts doing recon along our trajectory."

"What about scanners?" asked Chelsea. Like the rest of them, she was still getting her Earth legs, and she propped herself against FUBAR with one hand for support.

"Holograms don't fool scanners," said Schuster. "But thanks to running the reactor dry, there's not much left for them to detect. Any residual heat will be masked by the ambient temperature around us."

"Ambient temp'ture," Maggott groaned. "Is tha' what ye call this fookin' oven we're in?"

Ulysses grinned and tilted his face up to the sky, spreading his arms wide.

"Mother's milk," he sighed. "Been freezin' my ass off for two years on that fuckin' station. I ain't built fer outer space."

Quinn finished activating the projector and FUBAR disappeared behind a wall of scrub. The horizon was askew somewhat, and the overall effect was somewhat less convincing than the real thing, but it should be fine for what they needed from it.

Bishop shouldered a small fabric pack and hit the controls to close the cargo bay door behind him. It rose on its hydraulic arms until it clanked into place.

"Good thing the doors are connected to the battery," he said. "Otherwise we would have spent the rest of our lives inside FUBAR here."

Quinn didn't want to think about that, because it drove home the fact they had a perverted guardian angel. It would have been a cruel irony to make it off Oberon One, cross more than two billion kilometers of space, and get past an attacking force, only to die of thirst inside the ship once they'd made it back to Earth.

"All right," he said. "First order of business is supplies."

"Leave that to me," said Ulysses. "Once we get into the city, I'll let 'em all know that I'm back. Then we'll be rollin' deep."

Quinn scanned the horizon. They were about ten miles out of the dense San Antonio slums, as evidenced by the brown cloud that surrounded it. Above the cloud were a pair of Towers, probably a mile apart, looming over the city like sentinels standing watch over the lesser parts of society.

They were all still in their Oberon One prison jumpsuits, but luckily the vast majority of people on the ground wouldn't care that Oberon One was a prison even if they had heard of it. The fabric was specially made to resist sweat and grime, but they'd been wearing the same clothes for the better part of three weeks now, and they were all getting a bit ripe. They'd be worse once they'd finished the hike into the city in the sweltering heat.

But they were alive. And they had a mission.

Quinn found himself fighting an urge to whistle as they started off toward the slum.

THE CRIMSON SUN was low in the sky over the smog bank by the time they made it to San Antonio's sprawling downtown. Ulysses had begun pointing out the bald heads and shaved eyebrows of Southern Saints when they reached Alamo Heights two hours earlier.

"These ones won't know me, 'specially since my hair's been growin' back," he pointed out. "The greeners get the outskirts; the central areas are for the higher-ups. Once we get inta Monte Vista, I'll start sniffin' 'round, see what's up."

It was a good enough plan for Quinn. Meanwhile, he was basking in the familiarity of slum life. He'd been in plenty of slums around the world during the war, of course, but they were all on the front. It had been years since he'd been a civilian in the streets, and this was almost like a vacation for him, especially after two years on Oberon One. The throngs of people rushing by, the sounds of hawkers selling their wares, even the smell of sweat and smog and smoke—it all took him back to his early years in New York City. People on the ground didn't have much, but they had each other.

That's how gangs like the Southern Saints had come to be, and later to thrive. They were organized criminals, to be sure, selling anything that could make them money, including other humans and unsavory services, but they also provided for the people in their neighborhoods. Many a time when he was young, it was the gangs that had dealt with periodic famine by "liberating" shipments of food destined for the Towers. And when the Tower militias came down on their random raids, it was the gangs who fought them off.

Quinn was a Marine right down to his DNA, but that meant he was also a pragmatist, and if they needed to rely on a gang to complete their mission, then he was more than willing to do so.

Downtown San Antonio wasn't like New York, with its crumbling old high-rises and claustrophobic feel. It was sprawling, with plenty of space for the millions of people living there. The sheer space around him since they landed had almost made Quinn agoraphobic, after spending the vast majority of his life in close quarters, first as a child, then as a Marine and finally as a prisoner.

They crossed the remains of the South PanAm Expressway toward Jones Avenue, and Ulysses motioned for them to stop at an overgrown brown park with hopeful patches of green dotting the ground. Massive elms with split trunks rose into the smog, their roots breaking the surface like giant worms flushed out by a flood, only these worms were desperate for any moisture they could find.

"Maverick Park." Ulysses grinned. "I spent more'n a little time here. My name'll mean sumpn' here."

Quinn raised a fist and the rest of them hunkered down on the dead grass. Maggott had stripped off the top of his jumpsuit and was down to just his strap T-shirt, exposing his massive slab arms and pale skin to the UV rays that always managed to filter through the pollution.

"I'd give m'left teesticle f'r a pint," he moaned.

"Let's hope it doesn't come to that," Bishop said, his voice papery with dehydration. He took the canteen from his pack and passed it around before taking a shot himself.

They were surrounded, as always in the slums, by throngs of people who paid them no mind. Quinn watched as Ulysses wandered through the crowd, seeking out bald heads. After a couple of minutes, he motioned for them to join him in the center of the park.

He pointed to a group of bald men leaning against the crumbling wall of what had probably been a public toilet several decades earlier, back before the huge open latrines had become standard in the lower cities.

"Folla my lead," he said.

Quinn nodded. "Copy that."

Ulysses ambled over to the men, who barely acknowledged him. The others kept their distance, but were close enough to overhear.

"Gennelmen," he drawled. "How y'all doin' on this fine evenin'?"

"Y'need a shave, man," said a muscular dude wearing only a pair of ratty jeans and military-style boots.

"Yeah-bob!" Ulysses hooted. "That's what happens when yer locked up in space prison fer two years."

The guy scoffed. "Ain't no drugs in Maverick Park, dude. Y'gotta got to the Alamo, they got whatever y'want." He turned to his companions and shook his head. "Fuckin' tweakers, man."

Quinn felt a twinge of satisfaction watching Ulysses have to work for it, after all his bragging earlier. He had no doubt the stories about his status in the Saints were true, but these fellows obviously had no idea who he was.

Ulysses' grin widened. "I'm Ulysses Coker."

They stared at his hand like he was offering them a rotten fish.

Ulysses frowned. "*The* Ulysses Coker."

"Yer gonna be *the* unidentified corpse in a second," said another of the men. "Ever'body knows Ulysses is a couple billion miles from here."

Quinn saw a brief flash of the Ulysses he knew in prison, and for a moment he thought they'd be heading into a brawl. But just as quickly, the look was gone, replaced by that charming grin again.

"Guess m'hair's longer'n I thought," he said amiably. "Just look me up on your network. You'll see it's really me."

"Ain't no network access out here," said the first man. "Even if there was, y'all ain't Ulysses, so get lost 'fore we get mad."

Quinn stood and stepped forward. "He's telling the truth. We were all prisoners on Oberon One."

Ulysses turned and glared at him, followed by the others. Apparently Quinn had just made a major faux pas.

"Ain't nobody talkin' to you," the first one warned. "By the sounds o' yer accent, you ain't from here, so we'll give you a pass. All you need to know is we run this city, y'hear?"

"Man, *I* run this city!" Prison Ulysses was back. "Where's Peckerwood? That redheaded varmint'll vouch for me!"

The other Saints exchanged looks. "Peckerwood?" said the second man. "Peckerwood's been dead for a year now. Bought it in one o' the militia raids."

Ulysses scowled. "All right, then, go straight to Bocephus. We ain't exactly friends, but he knows me."

The men pushed off from the wall and crossed their arms over their chests. Each of them was chiseled and looked able to handle himself.

"Man, Bocephus only talks to Saints."

Quinn raised his hand. "Uh, can we have a minute?"

The others stood up and circled Ulysses.

"This isn't going the way you wanted," Quinn whispered. "Maybe we should move on."

Ulysses shook his head. "We'll never get to Vegas without their help. We gotta do this, and we gotta do it now."

"How?" asked Bishop. "These gents don't seem overly keen on extending any Southern hospitality. Can we go directly to this Bocephus you were talking about?"

"Naw, he's protected by three layers o' Saints. We'd never find him on our own."

"What are the options, then?" asked Quinn.

"There's a couple, but only one that's viable."

"What are they?" asked Chelsea.

"Well, we could sell *you* to 'em," he said. "I guarantee there's a big ol' reward for you right now, Doc."

She blanched and Quinn shook his head. "Not happening."

Ulysses rolled his eyes. "I know that, Captain 'Merica. Which leaves trial by combat."

"Seriously?" asked Schuster. "That's still a thing?"

"Brains can help ya *stay* in a gang, but it's yer fists that get ya into it."

"Are you up for it?" asked Quinn.

"Pft. I live for this shit, man." He unzipped his jumpsuit and stripped off his undershirt, revealing his copper statue of a physique. "Why ya think I fought so much when we were inside?"

He turned and sauntered back toward the other Saints.

"I guess I gotta prove it to y'all, gennelmen," he drawled. "Let's do this. I got things to do and miles to go 'fore I sleep. Which one o' you's gonna be the victim?"

The first Saint looked to the others, then back to Ulysses.

"You callin' combat?" he asked, incredulous. "Seriously?"

Ulysses raised his hands and waved them toward himself, inviting them over. "C'mon, I ain't got all day."

The second man chuckled. "You *have* been gone awhile, assumin' y'ever really were a Saint."

"Yeah? Why'zzat?"

"We play two-on-two," said the first guy, dropping his fists to his sides. "Pick yer man, and whoever's left standin' at the end wins."

6

"They can *see* Maggott, right?" asked Bishop. "I mean, they're not mistaking him for a tree or something?"

Ulysses shrugged. "Dunno. You up for it, hoss?"

"Aye." Maggott grinned. "As long as the captain is okay with it, o'course. It's gettin' a wee bit boring standin' around with m'thumb up m'arse."

Quinn considered it. As Geordie had pointed out, the Saints could obviously see that Ulysses would pick Maggott, and they weren't concerned. Were they just stupid, or did they have an ace up their sleeves?

"All right," he said. "But keep your eyes open and be ready for anything."

"Yessir." Maggott cracked his knuckles. "Let's go have some foon."

The two men walked back into the park. Quinn noticed they were drawing the attention of the crowd around them, who obviously recognized what was about to happen. Slum dogs had to take their fun where they could find it, he knew, but he wished they didn't suddenly have a couple hundred people looking at their faces. He didn't know if or when Chelsea's father would make their presence known to the public, but he'd rather not take chances.

Then again, if this was the only way to Vegas, what else was he supposed to do?

"Well, shucks," said the first man, looking up at Maggott. "Yer 'bout the size of a grizzly on his hind legs, ain't ya?"

He shrugged. "Name's Maggott. Who've I got the pleasure o'killin' today?"

The first man grinned. "They call me Virgil."

"Who y'all got for me?" Ulysses asked impatiently. "Let's get this over with."

"Oh, it's you n'me," said Virgil. He faced off with Ulysses. "I ain't takin' on the big worm here."

Maggott turned to the second man and shrugged. "Don't matter to me who I beat on. C'mon, ye ponce, let's see what yuir made of."

"Not him, neither." Virgil pointed into the crowd, and a bald man about half Maggott's size emerged into the rough circle that had been formed around them by the crowd. He was wiry and lean, with the build of a featherweight boxer. The man's eyes were black and gave away nothing.

"Seriously?" Bishop whispered. The others shrugged.

Maggott raised an eyebrow. "What'm I s'posed to do wi' that? Eat it?"

"This here's Shoo-fly," Virgil said with a grin. "Guess it's kinda fittin' that a worm an' a bug would fight each other, hey?"

Quinn didn't like the way the smaller man moved. With his physique, there was no doubt he was a trained fighter, but something about the way he circled Maggott, like he was stalking him, that set Quinn's teeth on edge.

Maggott seemed to have no such qualms. He grinned and raised his giant fists. "Let's dance, wee man."

Ulysses took that as his opening bell and drove a fist straight out from the shoulder, catching Virgil directly in the chin. Quinn nodded —it was a smart opening move, because it forced the opponent's head backward, throwing him off balance. Ulysses followed up with a left fist coming down on angle and hammering Virgil's nose. An even better follow-up, thought Quinn, because it immediately brought blood into play.

His faith in Ulysses solidified, Quinn turned to Maggott and immediately felt his stomach drop. Shoo-fly was living up to his name, leaping almost a meter straight up while spinning backward. Despite being almost two feet shorter than Maggott, his boot was now at the big man's eye level and caught him full-force in the chin.

Chelsea gasped and clutched Quinn's hand. "Don't worry," he said. "Maggott's taken on far tougher opponents."

He wished he was as sure of that as he'd tried to sound. The kick had knocked Maggott backward three steps, and Shoo-fly was back on the ground and ready to follow up. His next strike was to the inside of Maggott's knee, which prompted a bellow of agony.

"Bastard!" he grunted as he dropped to one knee, clutching the other.

Shoo-fly closed the gap between them and took advantage of the fact that Maggott had lowered his hand to launch a flurry of strikes against the big man's head.

"Ha!" Schuster crowed. "He doesn't know that's like punching a rock!"

But they were having an effect. Quinn saw Maggott's head weaving as he staggered to his feet, and it worried him. Even with martial arts training, Shoo-fly shouldn't have been able to strike with as much force as he was showing. Unless...

"Shit!" he muttered to his people. "He's an a-bomb."

Chelsea frowned. "A *what?*"

"A-bomb," said Schuster, nodding. "It's slang for abomination. They use it to describe people who've had genetic modifications, either in the womb or through gene therapy later in life. It's how Senpai Sally and the other Yandares were able to do so much damage with such tiny frames: unnaturally dense muscle fibers, particularly in the joints, make for—"

"I'm a medical tech, Dev, I get it. No wonder they weren't worried about Maggott."

Ulysses was in the process of a spin kick as Quinn looked in his direction. The sole of his prison boot connected squarely with Virgil's solar plexus, driving him backward a good two meters. He hit the ground full-force, and Quinn knew that fight was over.

If only the other one had been going so well. Shoo-fly leapt with ease and wrapped his legs around Maggott's neck, clamping them at the feet. His weight wasn't enough to pull the big man down to the ground, but it was enough to allow him to hang upside down and thrust his fist directly into Maggott's groin.

"Oohh," Bishop winced. "Even his grandkids are gonna feel that one."

"Vegas is waitin' on ya, Maggott!" Ulysses called, and Quinn heard more than a little alarm in his voice now that he could see what was happening. "Drop that little shit and let's go!"

Maggott had gotten sluggish, and his blows were having little effect since Shoo-fly was able to dart out of the way of almost all of them. The little man's black eyes flashed, making him look like a mountain lion circling for the kill. The other Saints were closing ranks to make sure no one stepped in.

"We gotta figure something out here," said Bishop. "If Maggott loses, we're screwed."

Quinn racked his brain. What could give Maggott the advantage? A grappling match would be in his favor, but he'd have to get a firm grasp on Shoo-fly to do it, and the little man was as slippery as his namesake.

Now Maggott was on his knees again, and Shoo-fly was behind him, legs around his neck, squeezing. At the same time, he had his fingers laced under Maggott's huge chin and was yanking back with all his upper body strength.

Shit, Quinn thought, his heart starting to race. *Shit shit shit. Think of something!*

Fortunately, he didn't have to, because the next thing he knew, Chelsea was yelling at the top of her lungs.

"Percival Maggott! Drop that little bastard and let's go already!"

Quinn blinked at her, stunned. Bishop and Schuster did the same.

Chelsea, on the other hand, had her fingers laced in front of her mouth and appeared to be praying.

Across the circle from them, the Saints began to snicker. One smacked another on the arm and said: "Hey, man, you hear that? This here walkin' tree's name is Percival!"

She's a genius, Quinn thought, awestruck.

"Percival," said another. "Shee-it, bad enough he was saddled with the last name of a worm. But what kinda mother hangs a name like *Percival* around a kid's neck?"

"Rrrrrgghhhh."

Quinn's gaze darted to Maggott, who was still on his knees. He tried to send the big man a telepathic message: *Don't let him get on the ground. Stand up.*

"Y'done stepped in it," Ulysses warned, taking two steps back. "I ain't responsible for what happens next."

Maggott reached up and grabbed both of Shoo-fly's hands in one of his, prying it away from his chin. At the same time, he pushed himself unsteadily up from his knees until he stood, swaying, on his feet. Shoo-fly still had his legs around his throat, and Quinn could see Maggott's face had gone crimson.

"Derrrggghh..." he growled. Shoo-fly's beady eyes were widening.

"Here we go," Bishop breathed.

"Drrrnnaa."

Shoo-fly was raining blows down on Maggott's head from behind now as Maggott clutched one of the little man's shins in each hand. Shoo-fly was looking less like a predator now and more like a caged rabbit.

With the pressure from the scissors off his throat, the blood rushed out of Maggott's face. His eyes finally opened again, and he sucked in a ragged breath.

"Dinnae," he rasped. "*Ever.* Call me. That *NAME!*"

Shoo-fly suddenly let out a shriek as Maggott spread his arms wide, each one pulling one of the little man's legs along with it, until they had been stretched to almost a ninety-degree angle. Quinn had a momentary vision of a wishbone snapping, even though Shoo-fly managed to stay intact.

With a heave of his mighty shoulders, Maggott hoisted Shoo-fly off the back of his neck and over his head, dropping him from his full height to the ground below. Shoo-fly's screams stopped when his head connected with the scrub below, and Quinn couldn't be certain whether the man was just unconscious, or, in fact, dead. There was a time when he would have cared about the answer, but this wasn't it.

Chelsea gripped Quinn's arm and let out a huge sigh as the crowd erupted in cheers all around them. Ulysses, meanwhile, strode over to Virgil's partner and fixed him with a glare that could freeze the Texas sun.

"Bocephus," he said. "*Now.*"

THE FIRST THING they all noticed as they entered the lobby was the temperature: it was like walking into a refrigerator, compared to the blast furnace outside.

Eli, the Saint who had brought them to the old hotel across from the San Fernando Cathedral, pointed to a row of dusty chairs that lined the wall opposite the crumbling reception desk and told them to sit.

"I don't *take* orders, son," Ulysses warned. "I give 'em. Unless you want some o' what Virgil got."

Eli quailed and held up his hands in surrender. "Nossir," he said quickly. "I mean won't you please have a seat while I announce yer arrival?"

"Better."

The six of them sat as Eli disappeared down a hallway. The only light in the space was what little streamed in from the orange sunset outside the lobby windows. Dust floated lazily through the beams, stirred up by their footsteps over the ancient carpet.

"I'm not one to cast aspersions," said Bishop, "but I would have thought that high-ranking members of the Saints would live in somewhat better conditions than ordinary folks."

Ulysses grinned. "Just wait."

Chelsea used the time and the light to examine Maggott's throat. He frowned the whole time, but Quinn was pretty sure he was enjoying the fussing.

"Yuir worried about nothin,' lass," he said. "M'neck's as tough as a bull's."

"I wouldn't know," she said, peering closely at the red marks under his chin. "I've never seen a bull. I've hardly seen *any* animals, for that matter."

"Eh? Why's that?"

She shrugged. "I grew up on an entire floor of a Tower. You'll be okay, just let me know if you start to feel any tightness in your throat. We should probably get some muscle relaxants, just in case."

Quinn turned to Ulysses. "How much collateral do you have with these people, really?"

"Much as we need."

"Don't take this the wrong way, but it didn't seem like it out there. And this place isn't giving me a lot of hope for what we'll be able to get from these guys."

At that moment, Eli appeared from the hallway and beckoned them to follow.

"Bocephus is looking forward to meeting y'all," he said. "We'll fix y'up with some sweet tea in a sec, too."

"Sweet tea," Schuster sighed, almost reverently. "God, it's been a long time."

"Rather have mint julep m'self," said Maggott. "A triple, hold the mint an' the julep."

Chelsea grinned. "So straight bourbon, then?"

He winked and touched a huge finger to his nose.

The hallway was low-ceilinged and unlit, and smelled of old dry rot. The apartment Quinn had grown up in hadn't been much nicer, but he agreed with Bishop that he'd expected more from the home of a gang boss. Then again, his own last home had been a cell that he shared with three other men, so who was he to question anything?

They stopped at a suite door that looked different from the ones surrounding it. Most of the others were wood, but this one was metal. Eli touched his palm to a scanning plate set into the door and a lock quietly snicked open. He pushed the door inward and motioned for them to follow.

Inside was even darker than the outer hallway, but now Quinn could hear sounds. Music, heavy on the guitar and fiddle. Bluegrass? Who still listened to bluegrass in the 2090s?

The music got louder as they reached a heavy scarlet curtain hanging from the ceiling. Eli pushed it aside and suddenly they were in a different world. Quinn had expected a suite of some sort, but this was at least three thousand square feet. There were sofas and chairs and beds everywhere, with two long bars that spanned the entire wall on either end of the huge room. Bright lights pulsed in time with the music, and people in various stages of undress danced in time with the pulsing lights. It reminded him of a nightclub where he and the Jarheads had spent some time when they were on leave in Dubai during the war, except this time, everyone was staring at them.

There were a half-dozen cortical reality chairs strewn about, with people who had transmitters taped to their skulls that sent images directly into their brains. Quinn had never seen one in a slum before; CR had always been restricted to the Towers.

Quinn glanced over at Ulysses, who was sporting a beatific smile. He raised his arms and crowed: *"I'm home, baby!"*

A large man with a pink sunburn strolled toward them, flanked by two very serious looking men, all of whom sported bald heads and no eyebrows. The one in the center was scowling, and Quinn saw Ulysses' mood change abruptly and soon he was scowling, too. A few moments later, the two men were staring each other down.

Quinn nodded to his people, a tacit signal to be ready to fight. They nodded back, including Chelsea, which Quinn found satisfying. She was one of them now.

"I hear Virgil din't recanize yuh cuz yer fuckin' hair's so long," said the man in the middle. "I see what he meant. Yer ugly n'all, sure, but how'm I s'posed to know if you's the *real* Ulysses?"

Ulysses curled his lip into a sneer. "Ask yer mama to look at m'trouser snake."

Oh shit, Quinn groaned inwardly. *Here we go again.* He prepared himself to move quickly.

A second later, both men sprouted wide grins and pulled each other into a tight embrace, each slapping the other's back hard enough that Quinn could hear it over the bluegrass. They finally broke their clinch and stood back but still held each other at arm's length.

"Ulysses Aloysius, as I live n'breathe," said the man, shaking his head.

"Big as life n'twice as ugly."

"How the hell'd y'get here?"

"Thassa looong story," Uluysses said with a shake of his head. Then he motioned in their direction. "I want y'all to meet my new friends. We been through a lot together; wouldn't be here if it weren't fer them."

The man extended his hand to Quinn. "Bocephus. Any frienda Ulysses is a frienda mine." *Mine* came out sounding like *man*.

"Likewise," said Quinn, taking the hand. He introduced himself and the others.

"This the one whut took out Shoo-fly?" Bocephus asked when he got to Maggott.

"Wee bugger got his licks in, don't worry. M'neck'll be sore fer a while."

He sighed. "Y'just don't get value fer yer money these days. A-bombs ain't cheap. Are you one, dude? No offense, jes curious."

Maggott grinned. "All natural."

"We actually just shaved a grizzly and taught it to walk on his hind legs," said Bishop. "Now, I seem to recall somebody saying something about drinks?"

7

The soft couch felt good under Quinn's ass, and the bourbon felt good in his head, and the shrimp *chilaquiles* tasted so good in his mouth that he honestly thought he might have died and gone to heaven, especially after two years of prison pseudo-food. He looked around at the other Jarheads, who all seemed to be experiencing pretty much the same thing.

"You know," said Chelsea through a mouthful of food, "I like to think that my years in the war and working on a prison in space made me more like regular people."

"Uh-huh."

"And then I get a taste of this kind of stuff again and I'm like, fuck all that, I want to be a pampered little princess again."

Quinn snorted a laugh and almost choked on his shrimp.

"Daddy!" Chelsea cried. "Come save me from the big, bad Jarheads!"

"Stop it!" he gasped, after managing to swallow what was left in his mouth. Then he lowered his voice. "Seriously, these people don't need to know there's probably a reward for you."

Her eyes went wide. "Oh, shit. Didn't think about that. Sorry, the booze has gone to my head."

"All right," Bocephus announced. He was sitting a few feet away on a wide, low sofa that would look at home in any Tower apartment, Ulysses by his side. "Now, wouldja mind tellin' me how in the name of Johnny Paycheck y'all managed to escape from space prison and get back to Earth?" He turned to Ulysses. "On a goddamn Raft?"

Ulysses looked to Quinn, who shrugged. "Your territory, you tell the story."

And tell it he did, from the initial encounter with the aliens who took over Kergan and Sloane to the changes on Oberon One that led to them inciting a riot, to stealing the modified Raft and driving the other ships into the surface of the moon, and finally to gliding their ship to an emergency landing and hiding it on an old landing strip at Randolph Air Force Base.

"So we gotta move, man," he said. "We 'preciate the hospitality n'all, but the clock is tickin' and we got shit to do if we're gonna stop these fuckers from takin' over the planet."

Bospehus looked at him, expressionless, for several moments. Then he looked over to Quinn and crew, then back to Ulysses.

"If y'all don't wanna tell me how y'got here, thass one thing," he said finally. "But don't piss on m'leg and tell me it's rainin.' Thass just plain *rude,* man."

"It's true," Quinn said solemnly. "Every word of it. Well, Ulysses kind of played up his own role in things, but other than that..."

Ulysses flipped him the bird and turned to Bocephus. "Man, if I had a credit fer every time I said this shit was crazy over the last six weeks, I'd build m'own Tower. I'm tellin' y'all, it's the gospel truth."

Bocephus seemed to consider that for a while before finally shaking his head.

"Look, I'm bound by my oath to the Saints to give Ulysses what he needs, but I'm gonna take a pass on buyin' inta this horseshit fer now."

"That's all we can ask," said Quinn. "And you have our sincere gratitude for all of it."

"Shee-it," he said, waving a hand. "Ulysses here's saved my white ass more times than I c'n 'member. I still think y'all went crazy in space prison, though."

"Sir." Schuster appeared beside Quinn with Eli in tow. "These guys have some seriously advanced tech. But most importantly, they've got palladium for FUBAR's reactor. We should be set."

"Foo-bar?" Bocephus made a face. "You named yer ship Foo-bar?"

Quinn grinned. "Yup. Fucked Up Beyond All Repair. It just seemed like the best way to describe our lives right now."

AT SUNRISE THE NEXT DAY, they rode in the back of a large cube van through the city, headed for Randolph Base and FUBAR. Ulysses pointed out the window as they passed the crumbling ruins of an ancient building. Throngs of people had camped out on the empty space in front of it, and some were even using it for shelter.

"That's the Alamo," he said somberly. "Never gave it much thought b'fore, but now I cain't help thinkin' about it."

"Why's that?" asked Bishop, hunkered on the floor between Schuster and Maggott.

"I think I know," said Quinn. "This was the site of a historic battle during the Texas Revolution, some 250 years ago. A small group of fighters held off the Mexican Army for a long time before they were finally defeated. Killed to a man."

Ulysses nodded. "Took a shitload o'enemies with 'em, too. Then afterwards, people'd yell 'Remember the Alamo!' and it'd get 'em all riled up to fight. They finally crushed Santa Anna and won."

Chelsea frowned. "Well, *that* cheered me up."

"We have to realize what we're headed into," said Quinn. "The odds are so stacked against us as to be a statistical certainty. We're going to lose."

"I'm with Chelsea," said Bishop. "You suck at pep talks, Lee."

"I think I hear what the captain's sayin.'" Maggott shook his head. "Sorry, sir. What *Lee* is sayin.' He wants us t'realize tha' we're already dead." He pronounced it *deed.*

Quinn nodded. "It's very liberating when you know you're going to die. You take risks you'd never take otherwise. When it's the last play of the game, and you see the defensive line barreling down on you, you throw that ball as high and hard as you can, in any direction, because you have nothing to lose. And if fate is on your side, it just might guide the ball into someone's hands in the end zone."

Schuster frowned. "What are you talking about?"

"Seriously?" Ulysses gawped. "That's basic gridiron football, man. A Hail Mary pass."

"Football's played with yuir feet," Maggott growled. "Nae yer hands."

"If I touched the ball with my hands, I got a penalty," said Schuster. "But maybe that was just the rules in India."

Bishop sighed. "Why didn't I remember to bring that bottle of bourbon with me?"

THE TRIP back to Randolph took considerably less time than their walk into the city the day before. Quinn guided Eli, who was driving, to where they had left FUBAR. Soon they could see a blocky patch of air that indicated the edges of the camo projector's hologram.

The truck pulled up alongside the projection and Eli killed the electric engine. They piled out through the cargo door in back, and Maggott carried out a metal crate about a meter cubed. The hologram disappeared and Maggott carried their supplies inside, followed by the rest of the crew except Quinn.

Bocephus handed Ulysses a tangle of wristbands. "These says yer all UFT citizens, and there's five thousand credits attached to each ID. That should do yuh in Sin City, long as y'all keep yer peckers in yer pants."

The wristbands were the standard form of identification outside the slums, linked to virtual banks and government databases via the worldwide network. They were essentially electronic wallets that could connect with bank and credit accounts, or be loaded with electronic cash that was carried directly within the band. Most people outside the slums did both, though actual cash was the order of the day in the slums, since charging the bands and getting access to the network were often impossible.

Ulysses took one and handed the rest to Quinn, who felt some relief at finally placing one on his own arm. The Jarheads were mobile now, and officially people in the eyes of the law and the world outside the slums. They would need that if they were going to have any hope of finding people to listen to them. It was tangible evidence that they had a fighting chance of completing their mission, and that they weren't necessarily fighting a losing battle.

He saw Ulysses and Bocephus embrace again, pounding each other's backs with their fists, as if to say "I'm huggin' yuh, but I'm hittin' yuh, too!"

"The South shall rise again," Ulysses said somberly. Bocephus replied with the same phrase.

"I can't thank you enough," said Quinn. "For the palladium, the wristbands, the hospitality. For believing in us."

"Who sez I believe yuh?" He shook his head. "I still think y'all got bedbugs in yer brains."

Ulysses sighed. "I cain't force yuh to b'lieve us, but just promise to keep yer ear to the ground, all right?"

"For you, all right. I will wish y'all good luck. Yer gonna need it in Vegas."

Bishop gave him the thumbs up from the rear of the ship. They were ready to go.

"I appreciate the sentiment," said Quinn. "But we're not going to be gambling."

"That wun't what I was talkin' about," said Bocephus. Then he climbed into the truck and Eli drove them back in the direction they'd come from.

Quinn and Ulysses boarded FUBAR, where Schuster was in the process of restarting the fusion reactor.

"What did he mean by that?" Quinn asked as the rear door slid upward on its hydraulics.

Ulysses chuckled. "You ain't never been to Vegas, have yuh?"

8

Schuster kept the ship under the fog bank ceiling from Randolph until it started to clear about two hundred kilometers outside the city. Staying low meant avoiding most of the air traffic, even though they couldn't reach the speeds of the ships at higher altitudes. FUBAR tended to handle like a saddled sow in the winds down there, but it was their best bet to be seen as just another cargo transport making its way between cities.

"Eli has quite a head for tech," said Schuster as he guided the stick, eyes on the screens in front of him. "He gave me a code to mask FUBAR's electronic signature as one of SkyLode's Rafts. Although I doubt any police would believe it even if it did pop up on the screens when they passed. 'Oh, look, someone stole a Raft from that space station prison orbiting Uranus and got it back to Earth somehow.'" They'd likely just chalk it up to a glitch in their system."

"Maybe," said Quinn from his jump seat. "But better safe than sorry. Why aren't you just using autopilot?"

Schuster grinned. "I need the practice. Plus it makes me feel like a badass."

Quinn snorted a chuckle. "I feel the need. The need for speed."

"What?"

"Nothing. Just a line from an old two-D movie from a hundred years ago. It was about hotshot Navy pilots taking stupid risks to show off."

"I don't remember that one. Then again, most of the old movies we managed to access from the public archives when I was a kid were made in India. There were a million movies about people dancing around, but not a single one about military aircraft."

West Texas unfurled underneath them like a blanket of white. Fields that had been home to huge cattle herds and cotton plantations were now long dead, dried up to hardpan by the changing weather patterns over the last fifty years. They flew over military bases that, like Randolph, had been abandoned decades earlier in favor of newer, shinier ones all over the world, thanks to the international military alliances that had sprung up first during the Trade Wars of the 2070s, then in the lead-up to the Trilateral War.

It was wide open space down there now, and nothing else. Miles and miles of miles and miles.

"That almost makes me agoraphobic just looking at it," said Schuster. "All that space."

"I like it," said Quinn. "You can see 'em coming."

"See who coming?"

Quinn shrugged. "Whoever."

"You're weird, sir."

IT TOOK them less than three hours to fly the two thousand kilometers between San Antonio and Las Vegas, and because of the two-hour time difference, it was only 8 a.m. when they arrived.

Schuster brought them in from the south, over Henderson, where the public airship hangars were all located. No one was allowed to fly private airships into Vegas proper unless they were an employee of the Las Vegas city-state with special security clearance. They pinged the air traffic controller and asked for a rental berth for three days.

Schuster turned the thrusters downward as they reached an

open-roofed hangar at least three hundred meters square. He maneuvered the ship over an empty dock, and lowered it into place. A series of locking clamps automatically rose up from the platform and attached themselves to FUBAR's wings as soon as the ship powered down.

"They're serious 'bout money in Vegas," Ulysses said as they prepared to debark. "Try to take off without payin' yer tab and you'll just rip this pig's wings clean off."

"We'll pre-pay, just in case," said Quinn. "We may need to get out of here in a hurry, and a wingless Raft isn't much use to us."

They stepped onto the dock's platform and Quinn was immediately overwhelmed by what he saw. The huge hangar was filled with some of the most luxurious ships he'd ever seen. Every once in awhile during the war, the Jarheads would get leave in one of the world's more impressive cities, usually in Southeast Asia or South America, and they would see some spectacular sights. But this was something else entirely. Their own berth was one of the smallest in the hangar; most of the others housed yachts that could easily carry sixty or seventy people.

"And these are the poor folks," Bishop said quietly as they walked along the gangplank that led to the hangar controller's kiosk. "The real money gets to park in Vegas proper."

"Here's where we find out if these things work," Quinn said, raising his wristband.

Ulysses frowned. "They'll work, Quinn, don't sweat it."

"And if they don't, we can always fight our way out of here," said Bishop. "Like we usually do."

An artificial intelligence hologram of a buxom woman smiled in greeting as they reached the kiosk.

"Berth Number A302," she said sweetly. "What currency do you wish to use?"

"UFT credits," said Quinn, trying to sound nonchalant.

"That will be five hundred UFT credits per twenty-four-hour cycle."

"Does that include tax?"

Ulysses smacked his arm as the hologram smiled indulgently.

"First time in Las Vegas?" she asked.

"Uh, yes."

"There are no taxes here. Whatever you win, you keep. Please present your method of payment."

Quinn raised his wristband. A green light flashed on its small display screen as a corresponding light did the same on the panel on the kiosk desk.

"We'll pre-pay for three nights," he said. "What's the procedure for departure?"

"Simply display the wristband that you just paid with and your ship will be released automatically."

"He always this anal?" he heard Ulysses ask.

"You dinnae get to the rank o' captain in the Marines without bein' a stickler fer details," said Maggott.

"It saved our ass many times," said Schuster.

"Can I get a receipt?" Quinn asked.

"Receipt," Ulysses sighed. "Shee-it."

A moment later, the wristband flashed green again and Quinn felt a wave of relief. The bands worked.

"Enjoy your stay in incredible Las Vegas," said the hologram. "The experience awaits."

"I'm sure it does," said Quinn. What exactly that experience was would be was anyone's guess.

The hangar opened onto a huge square that bustled with ground and air transports. Ulysses fiddled with an app on his wristband to flag down a ride to their destination, and immediately a large drone buzzed over to them. It was about twenty meters above them, but as soon as it was over their location, it extended four retractable legs to the pavement. Then it killed its vertical thrusters and lowered itself to the ground on its legs.

"Classy," Bishop observed.

Chelsea grinned. "They don't want to mess up anyone's hair with their downdraft."

The six of them climbed into the back of the aircraft—Maggott had to wrestle his bulk inside—and were met by another holographic face, this time a handsome young man.

"English?" it asked.

"Nothin' but," said Ulysses as he buckled in. His grin was a mile wide.

"Thank you. My name is Ari. Your requested destination is the north end of the Strip, is that correct?"

"Yep."

"Thank you. May I suggest a higher level of accommodation for a small fee? Something above the cloud?"

Before Ulysses could answer, Quinn said: "No, thanks."

"Excellent. Your trip will be thirteen minutes."

Chelsea leaned forward. "Ari, listen for your name."

"Yes ma'am," the hologram replied as they lifted off. It disappeared.

"What happened?" asked Quinn.

"If you don't tell the AIs to listen for their names, they'll listen in on everything around them," she said. "It's a customer service thing. But if you tell them to listen for their names, they'll shut off the audio receptors until their name activates them again."

"Oh." Quinn felt a flash of embarrassment. "Sorry, the only AIs I've ever dealt with are military ones, and they don't come with holographic faces."

She smiled. "Look, you got us out of space prison and back to Earth. Ulysses got us to this point. At least let me use my rich princess upbringing to help us get through Vegas, okay?"

"Like it or not, Lee, we're in uncharted territory," said Bishop. "None of us has ever been here before. Hell, none of us knows anything except slums and war zones."

"And prison," Schuster pointed out.

"You're not helping, Dev."

Quinn nodded, sighing. Part of this mission was learning that he wasn't always going to be the leader. He didn't have the luxury to nurse his ego when the fate of the world hung in the balance.

"So what do you know about Vegas?" he asked. "Let's take a crash course in the twelve minutes we've got left."

Chelsea pointed out the window as they rose above the smog into the clear light of the upper atmosphere. Towers covered the landscape, more than Quinn had ever seen in one place before. Many of them were taller than any he'd seen, as well, and a few appeared to actually be made out of gold, though he knew that was impossible.

Wasn't it?

"They always fly people above the clouds here," said Chelsea. "I mean, all upper strata transports do that so that people don't have to see the slums, but in Vegas it's a concerted effort to upsell you. They figure if you see this view, you'll fork over the extra credits for a taste of the good life instead of going the cheap route on the ground."

"How do they get away with nae collectin' taxes?" asked Maggott. His shoulders were hunched forward in the too-small seat.

"Vegas is an independent city-state," said Ulysses. "Not aligned with any o' the factions. That way, ever'body can come'n spend their money without fear o' getting stuck in a war zone."

"That means they make their own laws," said Chelsea. "Vegas brings in so much money that they use it to maintain services and infrastructure. Trust me, it all comes out of the same pocket. They just take it from you in other ways."

"Like charging five hundred credits a night for a ship berth," Quinn grumbled.

Ulysses shook his head. "Y'act like it's *yer* money."

"That autonomy has its pros and cons," Chelsea continued. "Since it's neutral ground, you can't be extradited if you're a criminal on the run."

"That's definitely a pro," Quinn admitted.

"The downside is that Vegas has the most sophisticated police force on the planet, not to mention the huge private security presence. You can have a lot of fun here, but step out of line and you'll be in prison so fast it'll make your head spin."

"Ellie told me on the commlink call that she hadn't seen any police since she arrived," said Bishop.

Chelsea winced. "It may be different in the older areas on the ground," she said sheepishly. "I've only ever been in the upper levels."

"I been on the ground plenty," said Ulysses. "Cops never come 'round 'less there's serious shit goin' down. Then they're worse'n the militias. They'll just open fire."

"So what I'm hearing is keep a low profile," said Quinn. "Which raises an issue we haven't talked about yet."

"What's that?" asked Bishop.

Quinn ran his hands down the front of his SkyLode jumpsuit. It was starting to look—and smell—like it had been stolen off a dead body.

"God, you're right," said Chelsea. "Ari."

The hologram reappeared. "How can I be of service?"

"Change of destination," she said. "Take us to the nearest outlet mall."

"Excellent choice. Remember to ask about our customer rewards plan."

They banked right and headed downward toward the lowest level of a nearby Tower. As they drew close to the landing port, Quinn could see literally thousands of people wandering aimlessly with plastic bags, bathed in blinding sunlight that was being reflected into the space by a series of huge mirrors, no doubt to play off the gold features all around them.

The drone landed without the use of its legs since there was no one on the platform at the moment. They climbed out, leaving Maggott for last. He managed to step sideways through door and pressed his hands into his lower back as he straightened up.

"Enjoy your stay in incredible Las Vegas," Ari chirped behind them as he lifted off again. "The experience awaits."

Chelsea looked at the entrance to the shopping mall ahead of them, wide and welcoming.

"Now you're on *my* turf," she said, rubbing her hands together. Then she glanced up at Maggott. "First stop is the big and tall shop."

9

Two hours later, they were in another transport, and the Jarheads were in civilian clothes for the first time in seven years.

"I think I did pretty well, considering my limited budget," said Chelsea.

She was wearing a sports outfit that hugged her body with a light jacket overtop. The men were clad in non-descript pants and shirts, also with light jackets. Luckily, Chelsea had been able to find deals where the cost of the temperature regulating tech was included in the final sale price. The spree had still cost more than three thousand credits, which was enough to give Quinn heartburn.

Ulysses clapped him on the shoulder. "I told yuh b'fore, man, it ain't yer money."

"We just spent more on clothes than my father made in six months when I was a kid," said Quinn. "It'll take awhile to get used to that."

"I'm just glad to finally be outta that fookin' prison straitjacket," said Maggott. "I feel like a new man."

Beside Quinn, Bishop seemed preoccupied, and not with his clothes.

"Something wrong, Geordie?" he asked.

"No. Yeah. Sort of."

"What is it?" asked Chelsea.

"I'm going to see Ellie in person in a few minutes. For the first time since our sentencing hearing." He cleared his throat. "I honestly thought I'd never see her again. It's a little hard to process."

The other Jarheads shared a look with each other.

"At least you have someone to come home to," said Schuster. "The rest of us have to live vicariously through you."

Bishop nodded, and Quinn could see the beginnings of tears in the corners of his eyes. He tried to think of a way to head them off, but Maggott beat him to it.

"B'sides," said the big man. "She'll take one look at me in m'new kit and dump ye anyways."

Bishop snorted a laugh and the rest joined in, even Ulysses.

"I dunno what's worse," he said. "You people and yer lame-ass problems, or the fact that I'm startin' to sympathize with yuh."

The transport descended below the smog line and the brilliant blue outside the window quickly changed to a grayish brown, which made Quinn feel mildly disappointed. It hadn't taken long to get used to the beauty in that rarified air, even though he was coming back down to the world he'd always known.

The traffic was much lighter down here as the drone zipped past old buildings and over streets clogged with old electric vehicles. The streets were teeming with people, though there were considerably fewer trash piles than most slums Quinn had seen in his life. Hawkers seemed to be standing every ten feet or so, selling their wares to passersby. A large proportion of people were weaving as they walked, either drunk or high on some of the many drugs that were no doubt available on every corner.

The holographic driver dropped them off at the north end of the Strip, outside a crumbling building called the Stratosphere that stretched up into the smog.

"I'm back, baby," Ulysses whispered as he took a huge sniff of air into his lungs.

"Yo, my friend, you interested in a cortical orgy?"

A middle-aged man with long white hair sidled up next to Quinn and held out an old-fashioned data cube.

"Party in a box, buddy," the guy continued. "A hundred credits. That price is just for you, cuz I like your face. Anyone else pays double."

Ulysses stepped between the two men before Quinn could respond.

"Lookit my head an' eyebrows," he said. "Been growin' in awhile, but you know whut they mean."

The man's eyes widened and he held his arms out wide.

"Saints business is none of my business," he said, bowing. "Have a good day now, y'hear? The experience awaits, and all that shit."

Quinn frowned as they watched the man scurry off up the Strip.

"I could have handled that," he grumbled.

"The box in his hand was readin' yer lil' bracelet," said Ulysses. "He was jes tryin' to keep yuh talkin' for another couple minutes or so, and it woulda hacked yer code an' stolen every credit you got in there."

Quinn felt warm blood rise in his cheeks. Yet another reminder that he was in new territory, and might have to rely on someone other than the Jarheads for a change.

"Geordie!"

They all turned to the sound of Bishop's name and saw an athletic woman with auburn hair pushing through the throng of people. Her green eyes were almost wild.

Bishop dashed toward her and swept her up in his arms as people passed by all around, not even noticing them. Just two more strangers in a city full of them. Quinn wondered for a moment how those people would have reacted if they'd known the circumstances that led them all to this moment.

He looked away as the pair mauled each other in that desperate way only long-separated couples can.

"That reminds me," said Ulysses. "I gotta find me some tail 'fore we leave this town. Two years is a long fuckin' time."

Chelsea elbowed him. "Why do you have to to spoil a romantic moment, you heathen?"

"What's a heathen?"

"An arsehole," said Maggott. "Ye shoulda assumed that. She was talkin' about *ye*, after all."

Bishop and Ellie finally separated and headed toward them, fingers locked together. Her eyes were wet as she hugged each of the Jarheads in turn, saving Quinn for last.

"I should have known," she whispered as she clutched him fiercely. "If anyone could have possibly brought him back to me, it was you."

Quinn bit back on his emotions. This was no time for sentimentality.

"Ellie, this is Chelsea," he said, consciously avoiding her last name, just In case anyone was listening.

The women shook hands and Chelsea handed Ellie a bag.

"What's this?"

"I thought you might need a new outfit after your long trip." Chelsea grinned. "It's the same one I'm wearing, just in different colors. I hope it fits; I was going by Geordie's description of you."

Quinn saw the emotion in Ellie's eyes as she looked in the bag.

"Thank you," she breathed. "Oh my God, thank you so much."

"Sure." Chelsea's smile faltered a tiny bit. "It's just clothes."

Quinn leaned in next to her ear as Ellie showed the new outfit to Bishop. "Most slumdogs are lucky if they can afford one new change of clothes a year. Buying them is usually a special occasion."

"One outfit *a year*?" Chelsea sounded horrified. "I didn't realize that. It's a good thing most fabrics are dirt-proof."

"And sweat-proof," Quinn nodded. "Otherwise slums would smell even worse than they do."

"You must be Ulysses!" Ellie chirped, taking his hand. "Thank you for helping Geordie get here."

He lifted her hand to his lips and kissed the back of it, grinning widely.

"Ma'am," he nodded. "A right pleasure." Then he frowned. "Wait a cotton-pickin' minute here. How'd y'all know where and when to meet us?"

Bishop grinned. "I emailed her last night on an old account. Eli lent me his terminal, and Ellie checked in on a public terminal here on the Strip. It's possible that the people after us are monitoring the commlinks, but I guarantee they're not keeping track of the activity on millions of old email accounts."

"Cuz nobody uses it any more." Ulysses nodded. "Yer smarter'n yuh look, Stretch."

"He'd have ta be, wouldn't he?" Maggott offered.

"All right," said Quinn. "I'm afraid the reunion's over. We need to get off the street and start planning."

"Got rooms at the Wynn," said Ulysses, wrinkling his nose with distaste. "Sorry 'bout that, but we gotta stay in a place where there ain't a camera every two feet, an' that means it's the old fleabags or nothin.'"

"I've never stayed in a hotel before." Ellie shrugged. "I wouldn't know a good one from a bad one."

"And I may be a rich princess, but I just spent six months on a prison in space," said Chelsea. "So I'm not going to complain."

Quinn nodded. "All right, then. Let's start walking. Next stop, the Wynn."

They pushed their way into the throng, Maggott taking point so as to push the crowd away from them and around the rest of the group. Quinn noticed Bishop and Ellie were still clutching hands like their lives depended on it. It made him smile.

A few moments later, he saw something that drained the smile away instantly. On the burnt-out remains of a Denny's restaurant, a public holographic projector beamed four mugshots out onto the sidewalk, each about three meters tall.

It was the Jarheads, and under each of their faces was a single word in large capital letters: WANTED.

10

They immediately headed west onto side streets, where the crowds thinned out to the point that all seven could walk abreast. They kept their heads down, making sure not to look directly at anyone coming toward them head-on.

"Well, that pretty much tells us all we need to know," said Bishop. "We're officially fugitives."

"You four, anyway," said Ulysses. "My face wudn't up there. Nor Doc's, neither."

"My face isn't there because of who I am," said Chelsea. "More to the point, because of who's *behind* that projection: my father."

"Why do you say that?" asked Quinn.

"It's not an official Vegas bulletin. It can't be; we haven't committed a crime here, and the city doesn't recognize any authority except its own. That's why so many organized crime figures from around the world have homes here. When the heat is on, they come to Vegas until it cools down."

"It c'n cool down any time now," Maggott huffed, mopping sweat from his forehead with the tail of his shirt.

"If I was to guess, I'd say my father called up his friends in the local government, and they asked whoever owned that building to put up that hologram. That commlink code underneath the word 'wanted' is probably an anonymous tip line."

"My face ain't up there cuz the Saints pump a lotta money into a lotta pockets in this town," said Ulysses. "They ain't gonna poke that bear."

Quinn chewed over their situation. They had to find Zheng to determine their next move, and they had to keep a low profile. There was no explicit reward attached to that hologram, and the streets were literally packed with people, so it was unlikely that anyone would be actively looking for them to turn them in. That said, a stray look in the wrong place might lead to that commlink call from someone who hoped to get something out of it.

What it came down to was that they couldn't take any chances.

"We're going to have to hole up somewhere," he said. "Ellie, I'm sorry for this, but I need you to be our go-between. If you can meet with Zheng and bring him to us—"

"Like hell," Bishop protested, but Ellie held a finger to his lips.

"Of course," she said. "Whatever it takes."

"I *like* this girl," Chelsea whispered.

"Sir," said Schuster. "If I could get to a public network terminal, I might be able to find out who's behind that projection, and maybe I could do something to alter our mugshots. Make us look less like us, you know?"

"Is that possible?"

Schuster shrugged. "It's worth a shot."

"Makes sense t'meet in a public place, anyway," said Ulysses.

"Why's that?" asked Quinn.

"Ain't no coincidence they they're broadcastin' yer pusses on the streets in Vegas, dude. They know we're here."

Quinn froze. That hadn't entered his head; he was too worried about getting out of sight.

"Do you think they know we're trying to contact the major?" asked Bishop.

"How could they?"

"My father is nothing if not resourceful," Chelsea sighed. "It's possible he studied your backgrounds."

"He wouldnae have to look far," said Maggott. "Our trial was pretty big news."

"All of which means we need to keep as low a profile as possible." Quinn turned to Ellie. "It means someone might be watching when you go to meet him. Where is he living?"

"The Bellagio. Low-income housing. He told me his pension had been reduced when he was forced into retirement. He moved here because it was cheaper to live than Shanghai."

"The Bellagio?" Ulysses let out a whistle. "That place is a shithole, man. Worse'n the Wynn. Ain't gonna be no cameras in there."

"Where do you want me to bring him?" asked Ellie.

Quinn considered it. "Ulysses, where's the best place to lay low in Vegas? Someplace where we could still have access to a network terminal?"

He shrugged. "Downtown. Get anythin' you want on Fremont Street, long as yer willin' to pay for it. But the crowds are thinner down there, and people are less likely to give a shit 'bout escaped prisoners. Hell, we prob'ly would be the only ones there."

"Name a place, that's where we'll meet."

"Golden Nugget's still standin'. It'll have network terminals, too, but they ain't exactly cuttin' edge."

"All the better," said Schuster. "I'm used to military ones, and they're all decades-old surplus, just like all our equipment was."

Quinn nodded. "All right, Golden Nugget it is. We'll keep our heads down until after nightfall."

Ulysses snorted a laugh. "Only people awake downtown before eight p.m. are the beggars."

"We'll be close to the door," said Quinn. He slipped off his wristband and handed it to Ellie. "Use this to get something to eat. Don't worry about cost, there's plenty on there. You can check into the room at the Wynn with it, too. Lay low until you go to meet the major."

She nodded. "Got it."

Bishop took her by the arms and pulled her close. The crowd

around them had thinned out to the point where they actually had some breathing room.

"I don't want to let you go," he said.

She smiled and stroked his cheek. "We'll be back together tonight. We waited two years—what's a few more hours?"

As she turned and walked away from them, Quinn found himself desperately hoping those didn't turn out to be famous last words.

~

ASIDE FROM A HANDFUL OF WINDOWS, the hallway that led to Major Zheng's seventeenth-floor suite was lit only by a line of infrared bulbs set into the ceiling that made it seem narrower than it really was. But Ellie was used to tight spaces—the apartment where she'd grown up in Montreal wasn't much different than the Bellagio. She supposed that made it a *shithole* in Ulysses' eyes, but to her it would always be home.

She caught her reflection in a cracked mirror as she passed, and startled herself. The new outfit Chelsea had bought her looked incredible. She could pass for someone on the lower floors of a Tower in such an outfit. It made her feel good, despite the circumstances they were all in.

When she got to Room 1738, she sucked in a deep breath and knocked. At the same time, she sent out a simple little prayer: *Please don't let me lose Geordie again.*

It took a long time for the door to finally open, but when it did, the face was familiar. He was shorter in person than she would have thought, and his beard had grown somewhat longer since they'd spoken on the commlink weeks earlier, but it was him. Behind him was a small suite with a single bed, a ratty sofa, a holographic television and a kitchenette.

"Major," she said. "It's good to see you again."

He looked her up and down sternly, and for a moment Ellie had the crazy feeling that police were suddenly going to come rushing out from behind the door and take her down.

But that didn't happen.

"What was the last thing Geordie Bishop said before he was hauled away after his sentencing hearing?" the major demanded.

She didn't hesitate, though the words still hurt even now. "He said 'Don't waste your life waiting for me, El.'"

Instantly, Zheng's expression softened and he let out a breath. "Thank God. It's good to see you too, Ellie."

"What's the matter, Major?"

"I'll tell you later." He took her by the arm. "This isn't just a crazy dream, right? They're actually back on Earth?"

She smiled. "And only a few miles away, waiting for you. Shall we?"

"Of course." He nodded, closing the door behind him. "If everything you told me is true, we don't have any time to waste."

She hooked her arm in his as they headed back down the way she had come.

"I can't wait for you to see them again," she said, wiping a tear from the corner of her eye. "It feels like some kind of a miracle."

Zheng shook his head. "I don't think miracles involve the kinds of things we're going to be talking about."

Unbeknownst to either of them, someone was watching them walk down the hall with keen interest.

11

The Golden Nugget was everything Ulysses had said it was and more—or less, depending on how you looked at it.

The building was almost a hundred and fifty years old, one of the original casino hotels in Vegas, and it showed. The center of the main floor had once housed a pool with an aquarium built into it, but it had long since fallen into ruin, and open floors above the pool area were home to a small tent city. Unlike some of the Strip hotels, like the Wynn, that catered to low-income tourists, or the Bellagio, which had become low-income housing, the Nugget and its fellows on Fremont Street had been taken over by indigents who couldn't afford to pay rent.

The bars and casinos were still hopping, but with a clientele considerably different from the ones who frequented the night spots above the smog level. The neon lights down below drew in the moths and rats of society, offering them a place to spend what little money they had on fleeting pleasures that they could only find here.

"Check it out," said Ulysses, raising his bourbon in the direction of a table full of young people a few meters away from theirs.

"What am I looking at?" Quinn peered at the people through the smoky haze of the casino floor.

"They're slummin' it. I can smell the money on 'em from here."

"Why the hell would anybody come here if they dinnae have to?" asked Maggott, hoisting a pint glass of beer to his lips. There were seven empty ones on the table in front of him.

"Toldja, you can get anythin' you want down here, long as yer willin' to pay for it. Them kids is lookin' for somethin' they cain't get in the Towers."

"Like what?" asked Bishop.

"You name it. Sex, drugs, underground cage fights. Illegal CR brings in big money, too."

"Illegal cortical reality? What makes it illegal?"

"People record themselves killin' some poor sap. Some folks'll pay through the nose to experience that without actually havin' t'get any real blood on their hands."

"My God," Chelsea breathed. "Why would anyone ever make something so horrible?"

Ulysses glared at her. "That's life on the ground, Doc. People down here do whatever they gotta do t'survive."

"They could've joined the Marines," said Quinn. He stood and strode over to the public terminal where Dev Schuster sat engrossed in a monitor.

"Any luck?" he asked, kneeling next to the terminal chair. The smell of the old carpet suddenly assaulted his nostrils and he fought back the urge to gag.

"Not a lot. I tracked the projector's account to one Tabitha Hyunh, a member of the city council. But I haven't been able to hack into the actual account to get access to the files themselves. It's got some seriously strong encryption, which means Ms. Hyunh has some resources. Of course, I don't imagine you get onto the Vegas council *without* having serious resources."

They had seen two more projectors on their walk from the Strip to the Nugget, though the new ones didn't seem to be drawing any more attention than the first one had. But Quinn knew it was only a matter of time before a reward was linked to it and they would spread throughout the lower city.

He just happened to be facing the open door to Fremont Street as Elli arrived with Major Zheng. The sight made him feel lighter, somehow. More hopeful than he had been. He tapped Schuster on the shoulder and pointed to the door.

"Forget that," he said. "It's showtime."

The two rose and headed back to the table. As much as Quinn knew the Jarheads wanted to make a scene reuniting with the major, he'd ordered them to play it cool. No attention.

Quinn and Schuster arrived at their seats just as Zheng and Ellie were taking theirs. Quinn nodded acknowledgement, and Zheng did the same in return, but he could see the emotion in the old man's eyes.

"Sir," Quinn said in a croaking voice. "It's good to see you."

"And you, son." Zheng looked around the table. "All of you."

"Chelsea, sir." She reached a hand across the table. "It's a pleasure to meet you. Your men speak very highly of you."

He nodded. "Thank you. Ellie told me that you were with them on their... *adventure*. I must admit, I was somewhat surprised to hear that."

"It's all a very long story, sir," said Quinn.

"Then we'd best order a round." He waved his hand to the waitress, a middle-aged woman in a dress that would have been too tight for her even twenty years ago.

"Nah, I got it," said Ulysses. "Yer on a fixed income, man."

"Sir, this is..."

Zheng raised a hand to silence him. "Ellie told me. No point in using his name in a crowd if we don't have to."

Quinn smiled and shook his head. It was a reminder that the major hadn't achieved his rank by being stupid.

"Ellie told you other things, I assume?"

The waitress came and they ordered drinks. Maggott downed the dregs of his beer and belched into his huge fist before ordering two more.

When she was gone, Zheng said, "A lot of things. It's pretty hard to believe. In fact, I have to admit that I didn't completely believe her until I walked in here two minutes ago. Which reminds me: what was my daughter's name, Lee?"

Quinn frowned. "Sir, that's... private, isn't it?"

The major's eyes were locked on his. "Answer the question. That's an order."

"All right. Your daughter's name was Lily."

"What the hell does that got to do with the temp'ture o' spit in Wichita?" asked Ulysses.

"Lee is the only person in the world who knew the answer to that question." Zheng closed his eyes and sighed. "You are who you say you are."

"Sir, anyone could have looked that up online," Schuster pointed out.

"No, they couldn't. We had already chosen a name when my wife miscarried at seventeen weeks. She took that name to the grave with her, and I only ever told one person."

"I don't understand what's going on," said Chelsea. "Why did you ask that?"

"Because he wasn't sure whether we were actually who we said we were." Quinn was suddenly hit by the memory of the vision he'd had on the surface of Oberon weeks earlier, when they were extracting the element that Sloane had needed. The memory of seeing his own face looking back at him in Astana right before Frank King was kidnapped.

Zheng nodded. "There's a lot you need to know."

The drinks arrived and Ulysses waved his wristband over an old tablet-style panel, adding a thirty-dollar tip that prompted a lascivious look from the waitress. He ignored it.

"I'd say *yer* the one who needs to get brung up to speed, wouldn't you?"

"Let him talk," Quinn snapped, then quickly added "please" before Ulysses could give him the stink-eye.

"I know that you came here looking for my help," said Zheng. "And I'm ashamed to admit that I can only add to your problems."

"What do you mean, sir?"

"There's a reason I ended up living here, in squalor."

"How *did* that happen?" asked Bishop. "A retired Marine major should have enough of a pension to at least live on the bottom floor of a Tower; otherwise no one would bother becoming an officer."

"That's just it," said Zheng. "I didn't get my full pension. They cut it by over sixty percent."

"Bastards!" Maggott growled.

"Easy, big guy," said Quinn. "Go on, sir."

"After your conviction, I started looking into what happened that night in Astana. When you were attacked. You said you saw someone who looked just like you."

"Yes, sir. It was true, believe me."

"I did believe you." Zheng smiled. "How could I not? You're the most honorable man I ever knew. That's why I had to do something to prove that you were all framed. I started asking questions about that night, about who might have known about the mission. How they could have known exactly when you'd be in Astana to change trains."

"I'm not following this at all," said Chelsea, but Quinn made a curt gesture to cut her off.

"The more I discovered, the deeper the mystery became," Zheng continued. "Finally, I went to General Drake with everything I'd learned. How there were records of black ops agents stationed near Kazakhstan, but no reason for them being there. Allusions to a private intelligence service with highly advanced tech."

"What happened?" asked Quinn. "Or do I even need to ask?"

Zheng shrugged. "Next thing I knew, my personal assistant had filed sexual harassment charges against me. A woman I'd worked with for almost twenty years flat-out lied to a JAG officer, and I was called in to either face court martial and risk losing all my benefits, or simply retire quietly with a reduced pension."

"That's awful," said Ellie. "What would make her do such a thing?"

His smile was bitter. "Guess who happened to win two million credits in the intra-service lottery five months later?"

"Christ on a crutch," said Ulysses. "That's some serious conspiracy shit."

Quinn's eyes narrowed. "This goes right to the top, then."

"I see we're on the same page," said the major. "Don't trust him, Lee. There's corruption at the highest levels of this Trilateral Government, and things have only gotten worse in the world since the end of the war. There's tension between the factions, poverty is worse than it ever was, food is getting more scarce. The last thing they want to hear is what you have to say about Oberon, and they damn sure won't want the public to know anything."

They sat in silence for several moments, Quinn's heart sinking deeper with every beat as he processed what Zheng was saying. The Jarheads had been framed, he knew that for sure now, which meant their return to Earth was even more hazardous than he'd imagined. If they couldn't get the government to listen to them, what hope did they have of preparing the world to deal with an impending alien invasion? Their Hail Mary pass was quickly turning into a fumble right before his eyes.

"There must be something we can do, sir." He tried to keep the despair from his voice. "We can't handle what's coming on our own. Hell, it's a long shot even if we have every person on Earth on board, but without someone to listen to us, the human race is already dead. They just don't know it."

The others looked the way Quinn felt. Their drinks sat on the table, trickles of condensation running down the sides, barely touched.

"There may be hope," Zheng said finally. "I can't say for sure, but there's one person who might be able to—"

Before he could finish his sentence, Major Zheng's head exploded in a spray of crimson.

12

"D*own!*"

Quinn grabbed Chelsea and dropped to his back on the floor, bringing both legs up and kicking the table onto its side. The others quickly crawled in as screaming bar patrons darted around them, heading for the exit to the street.

"We're sittin' ducks!" yelled Maggott.

Quinn held up a hand to silence them. He was waiting for a follow-up shot, but none came. No one else fell, and their table, flimsy cover as it was, didn't shatter under a barrage of bullets or electric charges.

"Hold fast!" he shouted.

The screams began to fade as the majority of people reached the door. Those already on the street had sprinted away as well, so that when Quinn finally hazarded a look around the edge of the table, he saw the area outside the entrance was deserted.

Then the lights went out.

"Chelsea, Ellie, stay down. Ulysses, protect them. Jarheads, follow my lead."

Ulysses wrapped an arm around each of the women and crab-walked them behind a bank of ancient gambling machines. Still no follow-up shots. Quinn trench-crawled along the floor under the tables, and the others followed, Maggott bringing up the rear as he struggled through the confined space. Twenty seconds later, they were in the general area where Quinn estimated the shot had come from.

Finally, another short volley of gunfire came—only this time, it was the overhead lights that exploded. The casino was plunged into darkness, save for the sallow neon streaming in from the street through the open doors.

"Why aren't they shooting at *us*?" Bishop hissed from Quinn's side. "Not that I'm complaining."

"The only way this makes sense is that someone's looking for Chelsea, which means they were sent by her father or one of his cronies."

"But why kill the major?" asked Schuster.

Quinn's frown was grim. "He was talking too much."

He risked another quick glance around the edge of the counter they were hunkered behind. Five shadows dressed all in black were stalking their way through the casino, and judging by the shapes, they were carrying shock rifles. He could tell these were higher quality weapons than the ones the guards had used on them in the prison: lighter, with better accuracy and capable of multiple shots before recharging.

The fact that these guys weren't ready to use deadly force on them, at least not yet, was more proof of a backhanded guardian angel.

"We need to keep them away from Chelsea," he said. "As long as we've got her, they won't try to kill us."

"You hope," Bishop pointed out.

"It's the only chance we've got. I need you three to draw their fire while I get over to Ulysses and the women. Watch for my signal and we'll force them into the center of the room, then do a high-low. Go."

The men scattered along the floor, heading in three different directions. Quinn heard the air buzz as the men in black charged and fired their rifles. Explosions of blue light crackled throughout the casino, but there were no screams as Quinn made his way to the bank of gambling machines.

He drew up against them and spun to find Ulysses crouched next to a pair of overturned machines. Ellie and Chelsea were wedged into the corner the machines made, effectively giving them cover everywhere except from above.

"Nice work," said Quinn.

"Ain't my first rodeo, hoss."

He turned to the women. "These guys are after you, Chelsea. I hate to suggest this, but there might come a point where we'll need you to be a human shield for us."

She nodded. "Understood."

Ulysses looked from her to Quinn. "Uh-uh. I ain't lettin' a woman fight my battles for me."

"Here's hoping it doesn't come to that. Keep them away from her, because the second they have her, you can best your last credit they switch back to live ammo."

"Why'd they kill yer man?"

"I have an idea, but I'd love to get my boot on one of these fucker's necks and get the full story."

"Now *that's* sump'n I can git behind. I'll be ready."

Quinn clapped him on the shoulder and shuffled back into the fray. The Jarheads had scattered and were likely using the bar and the other banks of machines for cover. He saw a cluster of shadows moving in the direction of the bar and realized that anyone behind there was about to be trapped.

"Your girl's over here!" he called, then immediately dove for the floor. He rolled to the side just as a clump of electrically-charged dust hit the carpet where he'd been, turning it black.

Now the cluster was advancing on him. His men's orders were to break cover now and stalk the enemy. Once they were in position, Maggott would bowl over the men in black from the floor while Quinn, Bishop and Schuster swung for their heads.

That was the plan, anyway. He wished he had a St. Jude medal to kiss. They could use a little help from the patron saint of lost causes.

He stopped behind an overturned table and watched the blue targeting lights from the shock rifles sweep the room as the men slowly advanced. The Jarheads should be behind them by now.

Then came the sound he didn't want to hear: a clunk, followed by a Scots accent whispering: "Ah, fook."

The cluster spun and let loose behind them with a barrage of shock fire. Quinn was stunned by the rapid fire; he had no idea the new weapons were capable of such a thing. Black holes appeared in the ancient wood cladding around the bar as he saw a shadow leap back over it. One of his men was taking cover again.

Quinn threw his back against the table and tried to get his brain into overdrive. This was a stand-off. Their enemies would eventually wear them down and simply walk out with Chelsea.

Then he turned to his left and saw someone in black sitting next to him on the floor.

His right fist was already cocked and his mouth open to shout when a slim hand covered it. Suddenly lips were next to his ear.

"Do what I say if you want to live," said a female voice.

All the tension flowed out of him as his brain struggled to process the situation. A crazy memory appeared in his mind of an ancient 2D he'd watched on the public archives as a kid, where a huge man in sunglasses shows up in a gunfight and tells a woman and her son to come with him if they want to live.

If he remembered right, things worked out okay for them.

"Who the hell are you?" he hissed. He couldn't make out any features, just a black scarf over the lower part of her face, and a knitted cap on her head.

"Shut up. Your men have maybe fifteen seconds before they get fried. When I give the word, tell them all to hit the deck."

"Why the hell should I trust you?"

"You got a better option?"

No, he didn't.

"What are you going to do?"

"I'm going to save your asses, if that's all right with you?"

It was.

Electric fire continued to blast around them as she drew herself up from her rear end into a crouch. She looked at him and the neon light streaming in through the door reflected in a pair of large, brown eyes. His mind instantly flashed to Senpai Sally. Was this woman a Yandare? Could the fates possibly want to fuck with him that much?

She held up fingers in front of his eyes. Five. Four. Three. Two. One. Then she leapt from her crouch and pointed something in the direction of the cluster of shadows.

"Eat the floor!" he yelled.

A second later, whatever was in her hand shot out a green light in a 180-degree pulse. It crossed the room, illuminating the men in black for a brief moment, enough for Quinn to see that they were wearing light armor and helmets.

And then they were frozen in place like statues.

"What the hell?"

The woman grabbed his arm and yanked him to his feet. "There's no time to fuck around, get out the door!"

"Captain!" Schuster yelled from across the room. "Orders!"

"Outside, now! Be ready to sprint!"

Ulysses, Chelsea and Ellie appeared at his side.

"Whut the hell wazzat?"

"It would seem we have a friend," said Quinn. The woman was already running for the doors. He saw Bishop, Schuster and Maggott following close behind her.

He turned to the women. "Are you all right?"

They nodded, and he motioned for them to follow the Jarheads. Ulysses turned to him.

"Our turn, man."

"You go ahead, I'll catch up and take the six."

"Whut're *you* gonna do?"

"Don't worry about it. I'm ten seconds behind you, max."

Ulysses nodded and headed for the door. Quinn gave the floor a quick scan and found what he was looking for: a nice, heavy leg from one of the overturned tables had broken off right where it met the tabletop. He hefted and jogged over to where the men in black stood, unmoving.

"I don't know what just happened," he said. "But consider this a down payment. You just fucked with the wrong Marines."

He squared his feet, wound up the table leg like a Louisville slugger and swung for the fences against the head of the first man. It connected with a loud crack. He followed suit with each of the other four men. They all fell onto their sides, but none of them moved. It still felt obscenely satisfying.

He jogged to the doors and out into the sultry night air and onto the streets. A few brave souls had started returning to the sidewalk across from the Golden Nugget, but no one ventured too close.

A hand beckoned Quinn from the alley that ran behind the casino, and he joined the rest of the group in the shadows there.

"What were you doing?" Chelsea asked. Her voice sounded on the edge of panic.

"Just leaving a message." He turned to the mystery woman, whose face was still in darkness. "Who are you? What did you do to them?"

"They were wearing electronic body armor," she said. "I beamed a virus into the central processing units in their suits and froze the servos."

"Servos?" Schuster asked. "In body armor? You mean—"

"Enhanced strength, yeah. The nanite servos read their body movements and move along with them. But when you send a big middle finger into their CPU, they freeze up and stop working."

"So they can't move," Schuster nodded. "Holy shit."

"It won't take long for the system to automatically override it," said the woman. "We have to get out of here."

"Look, I appreciate what you did for us," said Quinn. "But we can't go with you unless we know who you are. For a lot of reasons, not the least of which is your safety."

"I'm a friend of the major's. I saw your friend here walking out of the Bellagio with him and decided to follow. Good thing I did."

"How did you know Zheng?"

"It's a long story. Just follow me; I can get us somewhere safe."

She turned to head down the alley, but Chelsea reached out and took her arm. The woman stopped and turned back to face them. The light from an overhead sign advertising GIRLSBOYSTRANS streamed down onto her, delineating a face that was far younger than Quinn would have guessed. Her hair was bobbed at the shoulder, and her eyes were wide and dark in a café au lait face. On closer inspection, Quinn could see they weren't quite the surgically enhanced features of a Yandare.

"They call me Gloom," she said. "And I'm probably the only friend you've got right now."

13

Gloom led them in every direction through a labyrinth of neon-skirted alleyways. Some were shantytowns, filled with tent homes and people, others were makeshift casinos with food stands and dice games, bootleg booze sold from bars made of packing crates. As they weaved their way through the crowds, Quinn came to the conclusion that, no matter who it was, everyone was looking for a good time in Vegas.

They reached a clearing in front of a bland old office building, and Quinn held up a hand for them to stop.

"All right, I think we're safe for a few minutes. You need to tell us where we're going."

"Back to my place," said Gloom. "It's safe there."

"Where *is* your place?" asked Chelsea.

"I'm in the Bellagio. That's how I knew the major."

Quinn motioned for them all to take a seat on a concrete bench that he assumed had once been for public transit riders, back in the days when buses still came into the slums. A few people hollered in the distance, clearly drunk and loving it.

"Never realized how much I missed this when we were in space," Ulysses said wistfully. "The night. The freedom. Ain't nothin' like it."

Quinn looked Gloom in the eye. Up close, she looked even younger than he'd first thought, surely no older than twenty-one.

"You knew Zheng," he said. "Well enough that you'd follow him downtown from the Bellagio just because you saw him with a stranger?"

"The major didn't hang with many people," she said. "Nobody, really. It was weird to actually see him with someone other than me, so it pinged my receivers."

"What did you know about him?"

She shrugged. "Obviously not as much as I thought. I knew he was a major, duh, but I figured he was just some retired desk jockey who moved to Vegas cuz it's cheap to live here."

"And you were friends?"

"Yeah. I got a lot of friends around the world, but they're all on the network. I don't, like, see them face-to-face. And the major was nice. So many people here are just trying to get money out of you, but he just wanted to talk, you know?"

Quinn got the sense there was more to it than that, but now wasn't the time to press her on it.

"So you live in the Bellagio? That's where we're going?"

She nodded and pointed to his wrist. "I can hook you up with new IDs on your bands so that those goons can't track you that way anymore."

"Seriously?" Schuster blinked, dumbfounded. "I thought it was impossible to change these once they were set. I mean, blank ones, sure, but once they're programmed, they're set in stone."

Gloom rolled her eyes. "Nothing electronic is set in stone."

"All right," said Quinn. "We'll make for the Bellagio. I can't thank you enough for your help. You honestly can't know how much it means, and not just to us."

"It's the least I can do for the major," she said. "And when we get to my place, the least *you* can do for *me* is tell me why he's dead."

It took them them almost two hours to navigate their way through the side streets to the Strip. The entire street was effectively a moving wall of humanity that prevented them from having any real conversation, and even forced them to link hands from time to time to keep from getting separated.

Finally they reached the Bellagio, and Quinn took it in: some thirty-six floors, curved somewhat, with a crumbling cupola in the center of the roof. Beside it stood the ruins of a place called Caesar's Palace.

"I heard the Bellagio was sump'n else, back in the day," said Ulysses. He pointed to the huge empty pit that took up a huge space in front of the building. It was full of tents and people. "This was a huge fountain. Used to put on a dancing water show at night. Playground for the rich n'famous. Course, back then, people thought they was rich if they had a million dollars."

"Seems hard t'believe," said Maggott.

"Gotta imagine it back 'fore everythin' went for shit. Back when *everyone* still lived on the ground."

"Come on."

Gloom motioned for them to follow her around the pit. They walked under dried-out palm trees that had long since turned brown and up a cracked walk that led under the crumbling remains of a huge canopy over the entrance. The frame of a curved skylight still remained, though the glass inside was gone, likely smashed out decades earlier.

She led them through the lobby, where several makeshift apartments had been built out of old shipping containers, and down a hallway. Unlike Zheng, her place was on the ground floor. She stopped them at a cracked door under a buzzing red hallway light.

Maggott arched an eyebrow. "We all gonna fit in there, lass?"

She sized him up. "I think we'll manage."

The door opened on an apartment that immediately made Quinn think of the place where they'd met Bocephus in San Antonio. It was easily two thousand square feet, and it was chock-full of electronic equipment and terminals, floor to ceiling. A single bed loomed in a corner next to a small refrigerator and cooking unit, and the floor was littered with takeout containers. There appeared to be at least two bathrooms, and, like the apartment in San Antonio, it was blessedly cool after the hot night air.

Ellie looked around, wide-eyed. "You're definitely paying more in rent than the major was."

"I don't pay rent," said Gloom, taking a seat at a terminal.

"Then how do you live here?" asked Chelsea.

"The person who owns the building owes me a favor."

"Seriously?" asked Schuster. "You know the owner?"

"Look, a lot of people owe me favors. It's how I live, off the grid." She made a gesture with her hand. "Gimme the wristbands."

They complied, though Ulysses gave Quinn a suspicious look. He shrugged in response.

"You got a better option?"

"Seriously, why're those guys after you?" asked Gloom as she fiddled with the bands while working a terminal with the other hand. "Those people weren't there for the major; they were there for you."

"It's a long story," said Quinn.

"I got nothing but time."

He looked around at the others. They gave him the tacit go-ahead.

"I don't think we have time to screw around," said Chelsea. "And like she said, she's the only friend we've got now."

Quinn spent the next forty minutes recounting their story to Gloom. As the time wore on, her attention shifted more and more away from the work with the wristbands and toward Quinn, until she was facing him, her elbows on her knees, staring into his face.

"That's how we ended up in Vegas," he said. "We were meeting the major in the hopes that he could connect us with someone in government who would listen to us and not instantly toss us into prison."

Gloom's wide brown eyes bored holes into Quinn until he started to feel uncomfortable.

"Staring is rude," he said.

She turned to Chelsea. "So you're really Chelsea Bloom?"

"Guilty as charged."

"I read about you once, on a blog. You're pretty badass. For a princess, anyway."

"Thanks, I guess."

"I've done some favors for your old man's company," said Gloom. "He doesn't know it, of course; I deal with people about twenty levels below him." She looked Chelsea up and down. "Bet I'd be able to live on the top floor of a Tower if I turned you over to him."

"That's not going to happen," said Quinn.

Gloom rolled her eyes. "Duh. I told you, I don't deal in money. Besides, what the hell good would living in a Tower be if a fucking alien takes over my brain?"

The others exchanged a glance. "So you believe us?" asked Chelsea.

She gave them an annoyed look. "What am I, stupid? Of course I believe you."

"Sorry, it's just that, as I listened to Quinn tell the story, I didn't even believe it myself, and I was there for most of it. What makes *you* believe it?"

Gloom sighed as she went back to her terminal and working on the wristbands.

"Like I said, I read about you, and I recognize the Marines from the news a couple years back. You were all on that prison in space, and here you all are, back on Earth." She turned to Ulysses. "Princess has money, you have money, if you're as high up in the Southern Saints as you say you are—"

"Whuddaya mean, *if*?"

"—which means you could easily have disappeared and gone on with your lives if you wanted. But the major trusted you, and you got attacked by those guys in the tech suits. So yeah, I believe there's weird shit going on." She looked at Quinn again. "Plus, I get the sense that you couldn't lie if your life depended on it."

"Yuir fergettin' one other poss'bility, lass," said Maggott.

"Yeah? What's that?"

"We're all crazy."

He grinned, and she finally gave in and let out a soft chuckle.

"Well, then, you came to the right place," she said, sweeping a hand at the jumble of her apartment.

Quinn felt an ache deep in his guts. *The major trusted you,* the girl had said. Yet another person who had trusted him and paid the price. And now they had no options that he could see.

"Gloom," he said. "Do you have any government people who... you know, owe you favors?"

She wrinkled her nose. "I don't work with government people. You can't trust them as far as you can throw them. In fact, I wouldn't be surprised if it was the government that sent that hit team after you."

"No," said Chelsea. "That was definitely my father. I have no doubt they were there to kill the others and take me."

"What makes you think your father doesn't work with the government?"

Chelsea frowned. "He's a businessman. His companies may have some government contracts, like SkyLode, but—"

"Boy, you really were isolated out there, weren't you? Big business *is* the government now. The end of the war was just a merger, not an armistice. The Global Families run the Trilateral government."

Quinn thought back to what Zheng had said, about getting his pension cut for rocking the boat. There was a time when no member of the military would ever have to deal with something like that. Hell, if it weren't for the pension, three-quarters of the military would desert instantly. Why go fight a war for rich people if you weren't going to make enough to get out of the slums?

"Doesn't matter," he said. "Whoever it is, we have to get ahead of them, and we have to get our story to people who'll believe it. And right now, I'm fresh out of ideas."

Gloom waved a hand and her terminal went black. She scooped up the bracelets and handed them back to their owners.

"Brand new identities," she said.

"I don't think they were tracking us that way," said Quinn.

"Maybe not," said Ulysses. "But you 'member that fella in the street yesterday tryin' to read yer ID? You can bet the men in black were doin' the same thing while they was shootin' at us."

Quinn hadn't thought of that. He was a bit of a Luddite, which is why he had relied so heavily on Dev Schuster over the years.

"Ulysses is right," said Schuster, as if reading his mind. "They were probably able to read and record at least some of the data in the time they were in the room with us." He turned to Gloom. "We owe you for this. Thank you."

She ignored him and went back to her terminal. "Can your ship get us to Europe?"

Quinn looked at Schuster, who nodded.

"Yeah. Why?"

"If you can get me to Rome, I know somebody who might be able to help us."

"Somebody?" said Quinn. "Who's somebody?"

"They're somebody who doesn't want anyone to know where they are," she snapped. "So that's all you're going to know about him or her for right now, got it?"

Quinn sighed, and Maggott stretched his tree trunk arms, letting loose a herculean yawn.

"I dinnae know about you, Captain, but I really gotta hit the fartsack."

"The *what?*" Chelsea asked.

"Bed," said Quinn. He looked over to the living room and saw Bishop and Ellie already curled up together on the ratty sofa. "Do you mind if we crash for a few hours, Gloom? Head for Rome at first light?"

She frowned. "I do my best work at night. But I guess. Better than having you all fall asleep on me over the Atlantic."

They all carved out a spot in the myriad of chairs and other furniture, while Maggott simply stretched out on the rug. Within minutes, they were all breathing deeply.

Quinn got up and padded over to the terminal where Gloom was still working and crouched next to her slim frame.

"I'm getting in touch with my friend," she said. "Telling them what you told me. Don't worry, it's military-grade encryption. If they agree, I'll take you to them. If not..." She shrugged.

"Thank you, Gloom," he said earnestly. "For everything. We owe you a lot."

"Uh-huh. I suppose I owe you, too. If you guys hadn't made it back here, I wouldn't have had a chance against the things you say are coming. They would have just showed up one day and zap! My brain is fried. I'm rather fond of my brain."

He grinned. "Hey, can I ask you a question?"

"Shoot."

"What made you become so close with the major?"

"Next question."

So much for that.

"Okay, one more and I'll leave you alone."

"Promise?"

"You—you aren't by any chance a Yandare, are you?"

She looked at him and frowned. "What kind of stupid question is that? Why don't you just ask me if I'm a dragon or a vampire? Yandares are a myth."

Quinn grinned and nodded. "All right, I'll leave you alone. But remind me tomorrow to tell you about a friend of mine named Senpai Sally."

He sat on the floor and propped his back against the sofa where Chelsea lay snoring softly. Two minutes later, he was fast asleep.

He didn't hear Gloom mutter: "Pft. 'You aren't a Yandare, are you?' Maybe these people really *are* crazy."

14

"Tell me again why you draw a salary, Zero."

It was the middle of the night and Zero was not in the mood for Toomey's bullshit. He was in a noodle shop a few blocks off Fremont Street, surrounded by sweaty drunk riff-raff, and his head throbbed like a rotten tooth. Luckily he had more than a little molybdenum in his skull or he might have been seriously injured like his colleagues.

He got up and moved into a filthy stall in the bathroom in the hopes of dampening the noise around him and to make sure no one was looking in on the commlink call. He sat on the lidless toilet and let out a deep sigh.

"There," he said. "Can you hear me better now?"

"Much," said Toomey, his face stern, as usual.

"Good." Zero raised his middle finger at the hologram. "Go fuck yourself. I told you I didn't need those idiots. I had to haul their unconscious asses into a basement after they got away. If I had handled that extraction myself, I'd have Chelsea Bloom with me right now and the Jarheads would be dead."

"Mm. As my father used to say, if ifs and buts were candy and nuts, we'd all have a very merry Christmas. The only salient fact here is that the woman is not in custody. Your job is to remedy that situation. If you're unequal to the task, tell me and I'll find someone who is."

Zero snorted a laugh. He knew he was the best in the business, and that Toomey was blowing smoke. Yes, all Toomey had to do was call the feds and tell them that Zero was a cyborg and he'd be in a cell within an hour, but that was never going to happen. Zero knew far too much for that to happen.

In any case, arguing wasn't worth the time right now. But he did want some answers, so he was definitely in the mood for questions.

"Quinn was asking Zheng about Astana last night," he said.

"Of course he was. Why else would he be back? He's trying to clear his name."

Zero frowned. "About that. You never told me how they managed to get off Oberon One and back home in such a short period of time. Or why they came back with Chelsea Bloom and a high-ranking member of the Southern Saints."

"I don't know how they got back so quickly," Toomey snapped. "Dev Schuster has a tested IQ of 180; perhaps he was able to modify the ship. As for the Bloom woman, she obviously sympathizes with their cause. It's called Stockholm Syndrome. The Saint leader likely just happened to be there when they escaped."

"Then why is he still with them? And what was Zheng talking about, that people in government didn't want to hear what Quinn had to say about Oberon One?"

Toomey scowled. "I don't know, Zero! Perhaps they were treated poorly in the prison! What does it matter?"

Zero was silent for a few moments. He should have known better than to expect more from Toomey. The guy wouldn't say shit if he had a mouthful.

"All right," he sighed. "I guess you're right."

"Do you know what their next move is?" asked Toomey.

"No, but they're going to get out of Las Vegas. Bloom had someone put up wanted holograms all over the lowtown. I imagine a reward will come next, which means that a lot of people will suddenly be very interested in them."

"That means nothing if you don't know what their destination will be."

"I don't need to know their destination," Zero said with a grin. He called up a display on the wrist gear of his tech suit. It flashed a receipt for Berth A302 at the Henderson public hangar. And the ship in that berth wasn't going anywhere unless he said so.

All he had to do was wait for them to show up.

~

He couldn't believe his luck. Not only was Chelsea Bloom standing less than twenty meters from him, she was *alone*.

Zero ambled over to where she stood on the platform that led into the hangar. A small crowd of tourists milled about, but because it was noon and the hottest time of the day, the majority of people had retreated indoors. He could see a sheen of sweat on the Bloom woman's brow as she scanned the hangar nervously, obviously looking for something.

That's my cue.

He took a deep breath and glanced at screen on his wristband that showed his electronic reflection. He'd adjusted the look with footage he'd taken last night during the raid on the Golden Nugget. He adjusted the hair and thinned out the face somewhat, since two years of prison food had obviously taken its toll on Quinn.

When he was positive his look was as good as it was going to get, he stepped out from his position behind a wall near the kiosk.

"Everything okay?" he asked, walking toward Chelsea.

She saw him and her face was suddenly awash in relief.

"Thank God," she sighed. "I thought I'd lost you in the crowd."

"Sorry." He tried to grin sheepishly. "I got distracted. Where are the others?"

"They're still with the drone transport," she said, giving him a quizzical look. "Where else would they be?"

"Just being anal," he said. "You know me."

He *assumed* the woman knew Quinn, anyway; they'd escaped from Oberon One and spent three weeks locked in a spaceship together.

"We should get the Raft unlocked and get in before they get here," she said. "That way we can be ready to take off as soon as they're on board."

Zero nodded Quinn's head. "Of course. Do you have the course coordinates?"

She gave him another odd look, and he knew he was making her suspicious. But what else could he do? He had no idea what their plans were. Thanks to the incompetence of his companions the night before, they'd had a good twelve hours to plan before he stumbled on them here at the hangar.

"It's just Sydney," she said with a shrug. "The simplest map program in the autopilot would get us there easily enough."

He nodded again. "Sorry. Just nervous, I guess."

"Don't be." She touched his cheek. "Everything's going to work out. Believe me."

Oh, I believe you, he thought.

She scanned the area again, and he wondered what she was looking for. The other Jarheads, he assumed. But he had to come up with a way to cleave her off from the rest of them, and she'd just given him an idea of how to do just that.

"Let's get over to the berth," he said, taking her by the arm. "We can get her untethered, even start the engines. Then we'll be ready to take off. Sydney, here we come."

"I can't wait," she sighed. "Finally! The ocean, good hotels, and no one after us!"

He grinned. *If you only knew.*

They reached A302 and Zero waved his wristband over the panel next to the gangplank. He'd transferred all the info he'd lifted from Quinn's last night into his own, and it worked perfectly. The mooring cables detached and retracted back into the hangar floor, releasing their ship for takeoff.

Zero had logged thousands of hours on a Raft in his career, so he had no concerns about flying it. Once he got the Bloom woman inside, he simply had to close the door, lock her in and set course for San Francisco and her father. If he'd had the time, he would have left her there for a while and gone to a casino to see if he could extend this lucky streak to the games. Not that he needed the money; he just liked winning.

The woman walked across the gangplank and through the open hatch. Zero took a step forward himself and then felt a sharp jab under his back ribs.

"How's the head?" a voice hissed in his ear.

He spun to see his own face looking passively back at him, only unlike himself, this Quinn had a Kelly QR32 pistol in his right hand and it was pointed at Zero's belly.

"Now, this thing is going to make some noise," Quinn said calmly. "So I'd rather not use it. And at this range, even with that tech suit under your clothes, you're going to feel it. So how about we both do each other a favor and you just get the fuck out of here?"

Zero's stomach sank as he realized he'd been led into a trap.

"No more red glow in your right eye?" Quinn asked with mild curiosity. "Must've gotten an upgrade since the last time I saw you. That was on the news. General Drake's acceptance speech on election day a couple years ago, remember? Of course, you wore someone else's face that day, but I never forget a red eye glow."

"Christ on a crutch." A copper-skinned man with extremely short eyebrows emerged from behind Quinn, also carrying a pistol at his hip. "I though yuh was outta yer cotton-pickin' mind, Quinn. But here he is, jest as ugly as you are."

"How—" Zero began, but Quinn held up his empty hand to stop him.

"For a long time I thought you were a figment of my imagination," he said. "A hallucination I had the night you stole Frank King from us. But a few weeks ago, I had an experience that made me think otherwise. Talking with the major last night put a lot of pieces in place, too."

"I helped a bit," said a slim young woman in a tight outfit with a hood that covered most of her head. "I figured out this morning that some of the info from Quinn's wristband had been read last night. Then we realized that, after I changed his, we had no way of releasing the ship because we didn't have the original band that had paid for it."

Quinn grinned. "So I hoped that you'd show up with my face and the info and try to steal the ship. I assume your plan was to wait and get me alone, kill me and then the others, and finally take Chelsea back to her father."

Zero snarled silently. He wasn't going to give away any information.

"Then I figured we might as well save you the trouble," said a tall, lean man he recognized as Geordie Bishop. He and the other two, Schuster and the giant, Maggott, emerged from around a corner at the same time. The redheaded woman from last night, who had led Zheng into the Golden Nugget, stood beside them.

"They sent me alone to meet you," Chelsea Bloom said from the hatch of the Raft. "So much less messy than killing all my friends."

"And here we are," said Quinn. To the others: "All aboard."

"Y'need some help, sir?" the giant asked.

"I got it, big guy."

The others passed by Zero on their way across the gangplank, making sure to flash sarcastic smiles his way as they did, and Maggott gave him a powerful elbow to the ribs. Schuster paused and stared at his face as he approached.

"Is it nanites under the skin?" he asked, tilting his head. "I bet it's nanites, combined with genetically modified epidermis cells. Right?"

Zero felt acid rise in his stomach as his anger took hold. Schuster caught the look on his face and hurried down the gangplank.

"This doesn't end here," Zero growled.

Quinn flexed his hand over the pistol as a reminder it was still aimed at Zero.

"It could, if I wanted it to," he said. "But I don't. And not just because I want to know what happened to Frank King. I'm keeping you alive because, as hard as this is for me to believe, I think I'll need you in the war to come."

What? Zero's eyes narrowed.

"What the hell are you talking about?"

"There's something coming. Something worse than you can imagine, and it's going to take everything that this planet has to stop it. That's why we're here."

He scoffed. "You're insane."

"Maybe," Quinn said with an odd grin. "And there's a whole lot more we need to talk about. I don't know who was behind you framing us for what happened in Astana, but I do know it was someone in a position of power. And right now, all I know is that you're smart and resourceful, and there's going to come a time, very soon, when the world will need every smart, resourceful person they can get their hands on." He locked eyes with Zero. "Even cyborgs. Hell, *especially* cyborgs. Think about that until we meet again."

Quinn kept the pistol trained on him as he passed and headed across the gangplank. A moment later, the ship's engines fired up, and the noise of the engines began to drown out the ambient sounds around them.

"That's not going to happen!" Zero yelled. "The next time we meet, I'm going to kill you!"

Quinn gave him one last cold smile.

"Zheng was like a father to me. Ask yourself why I didn't just kill you. I could have done it easily, even without the pistol."

A moment later, the hatch closed behind him and the Raft rose into the air.

Zero never thought to wonder why the ship's thrusters didn't kick up the dust and litter underneath it as it lifted off. Instead, he simply watched it disappear into the smog, his teeth grinding together.

And he couldn't get Quinn's words out of his head: *Something worse than you can imagine.*

15

It was noon in San Francisco and the morning fog over the bay had long since dissipated, leaving it, and the city beyond, awash in golden sunlight. Morley Drake could feel it on the creased skin of his face, on his ears, in his eyes. In the old days, when he was a schoolboy on the streets of Old Philadelphia and sweat-resistant clothes were just a distant science fiction fantasy, his neck would be itching by now, rubbed red by the prickly heat. As it was, he was cool and dry and comfortable.

And that was how he liked it.

He'd spent decades mired in crotch sweat, tromping through war zones throughout the southern hemisphere. Africa, South and Central America, Southeast Asia, even New Orleans right here in America. He went where the fighting was, because he knew, at the end of the road, there would be a better life.

He couldn't have imagined this, here, now, back in those days, of course. Walking along the waterfront, the polished concrete paths sparkling clean, the air so clear you could see ships flying over the harbor from miles out. Yes, San Francisco was truly paradise on Earth.

It was his home now, and it was going to stay that way.

He stopped at a food shuttle selling fresh auto-steamed Dungeness crab, and he bought a takeout container of it. The order came with a side of real dairy butter, not the oil by-product that was the standard these days, now that cattle were confined to preserves.

Drake tried to wave his wristband over the shuttle's tablet panel, but the plump middle-aged woman who had served him smiled and gently pushed his hand away.

"Your credits are no good here, Mr. Tribune," she said with a conspiratorial wink. "This world has a few generations to go before we've paid back what we owe you."

He smiled sheepishly and gave her a quick bow. "You honor me, young lady."

"Oh, you!" she cackled, waving at him again, and he winked at her before grabbing a polycarbonate fork and heading off with his treat.

He'd only gone a half a block before he heard a familiar voice behind him.

"Eating arthropods fascinates me."

Drake sighed. He'd only gotten a few bites. Goddamn it.

"Why is that, Dr. Toomey?" He turned to face the man, who always managed to look sallow, even though he, like Drake, lived in the sunniest city on Earth.

"You pull them from the sea, call them crustaceans and people will pay vast sums for them," said Toomey. "But serve those same people a plate of the crustacean's land-dwelling cousins—millipedes, scorpions and the like—and they will run screaming in the other direction."

"God, you're a fun date," Drake sighed as he pitched the rest of his container in a nearby incinerator can. It disappeared in a red flash almost instantly. "I assume you asked to meet for a reason other than to critique my lunch."

"Napoleon Quinn and the other three Jarheads are back on Earth."

Drake's world turned upside down, and he was suddenly very glad he didn't have a mouthful of food; if he had, he very likely would have choked to death on it. It took all of his military training and war experience to keep his utter shock from showing on his face. He looked at Toomey with wide, blazing eyes.

"*What* did you say?"

"I said Napoleon Quinn and the men who went to prison with him are back on Earth."

Drake felt his cheeks glowing red, and a vein began to pulse in his temple.

"I meant *explain* yourself, not repeat yourself," he hissed through gritted teeth. "What the hell are you talking about?"

"They escaped from Oberon One just over three weeks ago, stealing a Raft after inciting a riot."

His mind and his heart were sprinting against each other toward the finish line, and for the first time in years, Drake actually felt sweat forming on the back of his neck, under his shirt collar. *Quinn. On Earth.* He would dismiss it as a joke, except for two glaring problems: first, Dr. Toomey was incapable of joking. And second, if anyone could have broken out of a space prison, it was Quinn and his team of Marines.

"And how did you find this out?" he croaked.

"Oscar Bloom told me. His daughter is with them."

The colors of the clear afternoon sky suddenly changed and Drake felt his balance start to shift. Along with it came a tightness in his chest that threatened to send him to the ground. He fumbled in the breast pocket of his suit before managing to free a small, oblong metal container. He shoved the tip of it into his mouth, under the tongue, and automatic sensors triggered a measured dose of nitroglycerin to spray under his tongue.

Toomey frowned as Drake propped himself against a nearby park bench, his chest heaving, his breathing labored.

"Are you all right?"

"Jesus wept, you fucking ghoul," Drake panted. "No, I am fucking *not* all right. I'm as far from all right as Napoleon Quinn is from Oberon One. How in the hell did he end up with Bloom's daughter?"

Toomey relayed a story of Chelsea Bloom falling for Quinn and his story of being innocent, of defying her father and joining the Jarheads, of trying to meet with Major Zheng in Las Vegas.

"Fuck me," Drake breathed, wiping a hand down his face. He motioned for Toomey to join him in the shade of a tree, away from prying eyes and his security drones. He had automatically killed their audio receptors the moment he heard Toomey's voice.

"What happened?" he asked. "Did Zheng tell them what he knew? What he suspected about the election?"

"My men got to him before then," said Toomey. "Unfortunately, they couldn't kill the rest without risking the Bloom woman's safety as well, so they escaped."

"What's being done to find them?"

"Oscar Bloom has put out a discreet private contract to bring his daughter back alive, but I have my men on it. I have no doubt they'll find her before any mercenaries do."

Drake glared at him. "Your men *are* mercenaries."

"They're government contractors. It's not the same thing."

"Keep telling yourself that. Just remember who funds your little softball team."

Toomey offered an enigmatic smile that sent a chill up Drake's spine in spite of the heat.

"And you should remember whose technology was behind the cleanup of this fair city when it was designated as the Trilateral Capital." He swept a hand outward at the park around them. "From privately funded research, I might add."

Drake hadn't forgotten, and it pissed him off whenever the doctor brought it up. Yes, Toomey had helped with the cleanup, but it had been Drake's political savvy and tenacity that had convinced his two fellow tribunes, plus three houses and senates in the faction government, to choose San Francisco. And Toomey had still been with Prometheus at the time, before that now-defunct corporation's Antarctic base was exposed and its secret operations brought to light. Before Toomey had crawled like a cockroach out of one shadow and into another, emerging on the government's doorstep and offering his services.

All of which was beside the point at the moment.

"Tell your men that, once Chelsea Bloom is secure, the others are to be terminated with extreme prejudice."

"I'm not a neophyte, Morley. Those have been their orders from the outset."

"*I'm* the tribune!" he growled, jerking a thumb toward himself. "I give the orders!"

Toomey sighed. "Yes, yes. In any case, I just wanted you to know before you heard it from another source."

Drake goggled. "Another source? Who the hell else knows about this?"

"Relax. As I said, Zheng didn't have the time to tell them anything of value. They don't know the reason they were sent on that train through Astana with Frank King, and they never will."

They better not, Drake thought. If Quinn ever found out that they had been set up, and that Frank King was kidnapped to keep him from learning the truth at the armistice negotiations in Seoul, Quinn would get his revenge. Not murder—that wasn't his style—but he wouldn't rest until he'd brought down the entire government. And his men would follow him through the gates of Hell itself to help him do it.

The government that Morley Drake had worked so goddamn hard to build was in jeopardy. The labyrinth of backroom deals, the shell corporations, the untraceable credit transfers, the payoffs, the work that Toomey's men in black were so damnably good at. All of it could come crashing down around him. He hadn't worked so hard for so long to lose it all to four fucking Marines who didn't have sense enough to just quit when they were ahead.

In the midst of his deep thoughts, a single, unrelated one suddenly popped into the forefront of Drake's mind.

"Wait a minute," he said. "How the hell did Quinn and the others make it from Oberon to Earth in three weeks? Even the fastest private ship I know of would take almost six, and that's under ideal conditions."

Toomey's look was unreadable behind his glasses.

"That's something else I needed to discuss with you," he said. "It would appear that Master Sergeant Schuster made modifications to the Raft while in prison. I don't know how, exactly, but I've been in touch with officials on the station. I believe I need to make a trip to Oberon One to investigate further."

Drake shook his head. "Not until this thing with Quinn is settled."

"I thought that was obvious. I'll need their modified ship if I don't want to spend months in transit. I was simply informing you that I'll be commandeering it."

Count to ten, Drake told himself, his hands balling into fists. He breathed deeply, not wanting to take another hit of his nitro so soon. He could get through this.

"I'm going to tell you this one last time, you creepy little cadaver," he growled. "I've had it up to here with you thinking you run this government's intelligence service. I get that we rely on you for some technology, but there are smart people everywhere, just waiting to be discovered. And I have no doubt that many of them would be more than willing to take orders from me instead of sneaking around doing whatever the hell they want."

Toomey's brows hunched down over his beady eyes in a frown. Drake offered a him a grim smile in return.

"And one more thing, Doctor," he said. "If you think your little black ops team is a match for the government employees I can send out against them, then by all means, let's find out. Whoever's left at the end wins."

The two men glared at each other in silence for several long seconds. Drake was proud of himself; Toomey had had this coming for a long time, and Drake was glad to be the one to serve him his comeuppance.

It was Toomey who finally spoke.

"Just to be clear," he said. "You're telling me I'm *not* to confiscate the Raft once the Jarheads are dead?"

Drake reached for the nitro in his pocket again. It was going to be a long fucking day.

16

Schuster didn't open up FUBAR's modified engine on the flight to Rome, though there was nothing else in the world he would have rather done. He knew he had only begun to touch on the ship's new capabilities, but flying a lot faster than the ships around you was an excellent way to get noticed, and that was the last thing they wanted.

So he kept their speed right around Mach 1.5, which put them over New York state just over two hours later, headed for the Atlantic Ocean beyond. Bishop and Ellie had spent most of the flight to that point cuddling and talking low, while the others talked about their time on Oberon One.

Suddenly Gloom appeared at Schuster's side and hunkered down next to his seat at the flight console. He felt a tiny tug in his chest when she ran a delicate hand through her hair and bent over him to see the readouts.

"It's boring back there," she sighed. "What's happening up here?"

"Uh, just flying," he said.

Hot blood rushed into his cheeks. *Smooth, buddy.*

"These numbers are wrong," she said, pointing to the display.

"They can't be that low. We should get that fixed before we get out over the Atlantic. Good thing I caught it before we hit New York."

"They're fine."

She looked him in the eye. "They're not fine, they're impossible."

"Nothing's impossible on FUBAR," he said with a grin, quickly followed by an embarrassed frown. "Well, technically, yes, I guess a lot of things *are* impossible on FUBAR, but those numbers are right."

"The ratio is way off." He could hear aggravation in her voice now.

"Don't worry about it."

"You can't have that kind of output with that little expenditure! We're going to run out of fuel before we even make it to the Azores. We'll have to land at one of the floating resorts, and that means being asked questions we don't want to answer."

Schuster sighed. "Look, I flew this tub from Uranus to Earth, I think I know how to fly her across the Atlantic."

"Yeah, and if you don't, we all die because of it."

There was something in the woman's eyes that was making him angry and aroused at the same time. He didn't know whether he should give in to either feeling.

"The engines have been modified," he said slowly. "I told you that."

"Modified how?"

"I don't know, exactly. I wasn't able to see the whole process, and... well, frankly, I never went to school."

She gave him a smug grin. "Neither did I, and I'm younger than you, but I still saved your Marine asses last night with my tech."

"Yeah, well, I've been a little busy fighting for my life in an outer space prison the last couple years," he said, more aggressively than he'd meant to. "Not to mention the five years spent fighting a war around the world before that."

Gloom's smile widened, which both delighted and baffled him.

"All right, then." She nodded. "There's the guy I was looking for. I'm glad to see he was in there."

Schuster blinked, baffled. "I don't get you. Why are you here with us? For that matter, why do you live like you do? With your talents, you could be in a Tower anywhere in the world."

"You say that like it's something to aspire to."

"Isn't it? Doesn't everyone want to get out of the slums and off the ground? It's the only reason any of us joined the Marines. We didn't do it out of some sense of duty to our factions; we just wanted the after-war opportunities and the pension that came with it."

"Really?" Her eyes glinted mischievously. "You all seem like quintessential military types to me. GI Joe Quinn back there probably has the UFT flag sewn into his underwear."

That made him chuckle in spite of himself. "You develop that in the service as a coping mechanism. Well, maybe not the captain, but *I* did, anyway. The Marines were just a way out of Mumbai for me."

A shadow crept across Gloom's face. "That's all the major wanted out of the Marines, too, and look where that got him."

Schuster didn't want to think about that, so he looked back at the readouts. The topographical map showed a representation of the New York Towers below them as they flew over the megacity and then the harbor. As they passed, an advertisement for the monument at the island base of what used to be the Statue of Liberty popped up on the screen for a few moments, reminding them to stop by on their next trip and pay their respects. Admission was only one hundred credits.

Then they were over the Atlantic, which would be their only scenery for the next three hours or so.

"Why does Quinn always tell you guys to stop calling him Captain?" asked Gloom.

"That's a long story," Schuster sighed. "He was busted down to sergeant after a mission in Sao Paolo, right before we were court-martialed. He punched out a local militia colonel."

She looked surprised. "Seriously? Quinn?"

"Yup. He might have been able to apologize his way out of that one, but the colonel was a member of the Almeida family."

Her large eyes grew even larger, reminding him for a moment of the Yandares on Oberon One.

"Quinn," she said slowly. "Punched a member of a Global Family."

Schuster grinned. It had been long enough that he and his fellow Jarheads could see the humor in it. Or at least not fall into despair over it.

"Almeida almost managed to let a Tower get blown up because he was a prick. He's lucky that punch was *all* Quinn did to him. But the brass and the politicians didn't see it that way, of course."

"Whoa," she breathed. "That's bad*ass*."

Schuster turned back to his monitor. "You're not the only one with surprises, you know."

She patted his shoulder. "There may be hope for you yet, soldier boy."

"Marine," he said automatically, feeling his chest swell. "We're Marines, not soldiers."

~

MAGGOTT LAY on his back on the floor of the cargo hold, snoring thunderously and providing a soundtrack to the conversations going on around him.

"How did you share a cell with that noise for two years?" Ellie asked, eyes wide.

She and Bishop had moved to a corner near the rear door and sat legs crossed, facing each other. Thanks to the technology of the Raft, especially the upgrades from Sloane, the interior of FUBAR was quiet even at half again the speed of sound.

"Not to mention a shelter for five years before that," he pointed out. "You get used to it. In fact, there've been times when I actually found it tough to get to sleep *without* it."

She twined her fingers into his. To Bishop, the feeling was the very definition of heaven.

"I have to touch you every so often just to make sure you're real."

"You won't hear me say no," he grinned.

"Me, either." She leaned forward with a leer. "In fact, I recall both of us saying 'yes' quite a bit when we managed to sneak away into the bathroom last night."

The memory still made him shiver. Two years without her had been hell, but he also realized how fortunate he'd been: at least he'd still had Ellie's love on Oberon One, even though they were billions of miles apart. Maggott's wife had turned her back on him as soon as they were convicted. He wondered for a moment whether the big guy would try to contact her now that they were back.

"Do you think Gloom's friend can help us?" Ellie asked.

He shrugged. "If you're on the top floor of a burning building, even jumping off seems like a plan. We don't have any other options presenting themselves."

"You guys say stuff like that a lot." She looked at him earnestly. "I really hope we can get to the point where we actually have choices, you know? Otherwise, what's the point? If we're always doing the only thing we *can* do, we might as well let the aliens take over our brains."

"Don't say that," he snapped, then softened when he saw her reaction. "I didn't mean that. It's just that... the experience is... I don't want to talk about it."

"Sorry," she said. "That's not how I meant it. But Mom's death last month really made me think about things."

"Of course it did. She was your mother."

Bishop had known the Rosenbergs since he was a child, and he credited Ellie's mother with making her into the remarkable woman she was now. Her death had been a blow to him, too, though he hadn't had the opportunity to let it sink in, with all the other craziness that had been swirling around them for the last six weeks.

Ellie brought her forehead forward so that it was touching his.

"That's not what I meant. I'm tired of just surviving, Geordie. Taking whatever blows life has for me, keeping my head down, struggling for every meal. That's not how humans were supposed to live."

He gave her a half-grin. "Then why do so many of them live that way?"

"Because of people like Chelsea's father." She frowned. "I mean,

I've never met him, but people like him have managed to take control of everything while the people who work to put them there get nothing."

"Careful. They used to talk like that a couple hundred years ago and it led to something called the Soviet Union."

She nodded. "I know that. It also led to the Trade Wars twenty years ago, too. I'm not talking about a revolution or something like that. I get basic economics."

"Then what *do* you mean?"

"There's amazing technology in this world, but it's only being used by rich people. Look at those men who attacked us, the guy with Quinn's face. Their suits and his face are revolutionary. Imagine what the tech in that man's face alone could do for people who've been disfigured?"

Bishop sighed. "I know what you're saying. Technology could put war out of business, but the key word is *business*. Helping people who can't pay for it goes against that fundamental philosophy."

"Mom told me a story she heard from her own grandmother once," said Ellie. "Nanny was a nurse back when Canada still had free health care, and she went down to a hospital in Philadelphia to see a $40-million ion laser they'd just bought for working on brain tumors. Nanny said it was amazing, and she asked the people at the hospital how often they used it."

"What did they tell her?"

"They said they hadn't used it yet, because no patients could afford the cost." She shrugged. "What good is a miracle machine if it just sits there?"

"Nanny was clairvoyant, apparently. That philosophy runs the world now."

Ellie tightened her fingers in his. "But that could change. I mean, look at this ship. You made it back from deep space in a few weeks, and Dev said that was just the tip of the iceberg. And the technology that the aliens have is well beyond even this. Imagine how it could change the world."

Bishop was silent for a while. Her words had sparked an itch in the back of his brain, but he wasn't quite sure what it was yet. They could dream about stealing alien tech, sure, but they didn't have that luxury. They had to stop Kergan from building a means to get their alien armada to the solar system. That had to be their sole priority.

But still the itch. Why? He finally sighed and pulled Ellie to him, laying a soft kiss on her lips.

"Keep talking about those dreams, babe," he whispered. "We're going to need every last ounce of optimism we can get, and probably sooner than we even think."

~

CHELSEA LOOKED out the porthole at the horizon, which was currently the Atlantic Ocean. They were flying east, which, according to the international dateline, meant they were headed into the future.

"We've got about two hours to Rome," she said. "I think it's past time we brought up the elephant in the room."

"Damn straight," said Ulysses, looking at Maggott snoring on the floor. "Somebody needsta wake that big bugger up, but it ain't gonna be me. Quinn, yer his boss, you do it."

Chelsea sighed. "That's not what I meant. We're going to need resources once we get to Rome, and these wristbands aren't going to cut it. They're tied to UFT currency."

"So we exchange it," said Quinn. Chelsea had assumed he was dozing; his arms were crossed over his chest and his feet stretched in front of him.

"That's a huge risk," she said.

"Why?"

"Because the IDs on them are a millimeter deep," said Gloom, entering through the hatch to the bridge and sat cross-legged on the floor next to Chelsea. "They're fine if all you're doing is spending your cash, but the minute they try any sort of transaction, then the network gets involved. That's why it's a good thing we're going to Rome: we won't have to worry about customs and immigration because it's a no-man's land. All it would take is someone calling up your ID and the computer automatically cross-referencing it to your mug shot on the network, and we're in big trouble."

"Can't you just hack them again?" asked Quinn.

"That's not how it works. You can change the ID attached to the band, but the cash in it is the cash. It's like asking me to fold the bills in your wallet from fives into tens."

"Mebbe we can find someone needs UFT credits," Ulysses offered. "Trade 'em for euros."

"That's not going to happen in Rome," said Chelsea. "The people who live there rarely leave, and you can bet none of them will be heading to any of the Free Territories after everything that happened in the war."

Ulysses shrugged impatiently. "I wouldn't know, I ain't never been outside the States. Well, 'cept for outer space. You know whut I mean. Anyways, I did *my* part in San Antonio."

"We'll figure it out," said Quinn. "Always do."

His calm confidence was enough to make Chelsea almost believe, but she knew they were going into a situation where they would have to have money. It was how the world worked.

She rolled up the cuff of her leggings, revealing an ankle bracelet that glittered in the light coming in through the porthole.

Gloom let out a low whistle. "*Day*-um, girl. That's some serious bling."

"My parents got it for me when I finished medical technician school. They probably wouldn't have given it to me if they'd known I was just going to enlist and wear it into war zones, but I guess the joke was on them."

"What are you saying, Chelsea?" Quinn gave her a stern frown that irritated her.

"I'm saying we'll pawn it in Rome and gets some euros so that we're not broke," she said gruffly. "Then we can think about whatever it is we're headed into."

The look on Quinn's face showed he wasn't happy, but also wasn't willing to fight about it, which Chelsea decided was a victory for her. Instead, he turned to Gloom.

"I think it's about time you told us what we're flying into," he said. "I don't want to be hitting the ground blind."

Chelsea agreed with him on that much. Just surviving on the streets of Rome was going to be a challenge, let alone trying to make a plan with no information, just because Gloom's friend liked their privacy. She appreciated the girl's help, but they didn't have time for politeness anymore.

Gloom looked around at the three of them, and Chelsea got the distinct impression she was being sized up by those large eyes.

"All right," Gloom said finally. "I suppose it's the time. You know I messaged my friend before we took off and gave them the bare bones of your situation." She shook her head. "*Our* situation. *The* situation. I mean, it's the whole fucking planet, isn't it?"

Quinn gestured for her to get on with it.

"Anyway," she continued, "he agreed to meet with us. Nothing more than that, mind you, but I think what we have to say will be right up his alley."

"All right," said Chelsea. "Who is this 'he' we're talking about?"

Gloom leaned forward with her elbows on her knees, as if she was so used to keeping secrets that she did it automatically. There was no way she was keeping this from the others around her.

"Have you guys ever heard of Foster Kenya?"

"No," said Quinn.

"Uh-uh," said Ulysses.

"Get out of here," said Chelsea, feeling her pulse quicken. Suddenly everything was starting to make sense, and she was feeling the first tentative steps of hope building inside her. "You *know* Foster Kenya?"

Gloom grinned. "Yup. More importantly, I know where he is. Rome."

17

They flew over France for twenty minutes or so before emerging back over water as they followed the Mediterranean Sea coastline south to Rome, which sat almost in the center.

The smog bank that acted as a ceiling for most slums was higher over the former capital than any city Quinn had ever seen. Outside the bridge porthole, they were engulfed in greyish-brown mist, lit with a hint of scarlet by the setting sun, yet the altimeter said they were still more than two thousand meters up.

"I've been scanning the network," said Schuster from the pilot's seat. "I can't find any public landing sites anywhere."

"You won't," Chelsea said from the hatch that led to the cargo hold. "There aren't any. I was stationed here for a few months at the end of the war. It's everyone for themselves down there."

"How are we supposed to land, then?" asked Quinn. He hated going into a situation blind, and he was also not overly happy about the fact that Chelsea appeared to know things he didn't.

Smarten up, man, he scolded himself. *This is a serious situation. Put a pin in that fucking ego and accept that you're not always going to have the only answers.*

"You can pretty much land wherever you find a clearing," she said. "It's easier on he outskirts because the concentration of structures isn't as dense. Once you start getting closer to the Tiber, you won't find anywhere that will accommodate FUBAR because of the ruins."

"You mean like the Col'seeyum?" asked Ulysses.

"I mean like *everything,* old *and* new. The war left nothing standing. Ancient Roman architecture, the Renaissance, The Towers, all crushed. They were able to stand for hundreds or even thousands of years, and yet five years of Trilateral War left it all in a pile of rubble."

Schuster called up topographical holodisplays that confirmed what Chelsea was saying. The largest area of open ground within twenty miles of the river was less than ten meters square. Quinn scanned the area for a long time before finally accepting the inevitable.

"Damn," he sighed. "I wanted FUBAR close, but it looks like we don't have a choice. We have to bring her down on the coast and hike in."

"Not necessarily," said Schuster, a sudden gleam in his eye. "Shit, why didn't I realize this before? The inertia redirection combined with the more efficient engines—"

"—means you can land with a lot less thrust!" Gloom called from behind Chelsea. "Smart thinking. It's almost like having a hovercraft in the air."

"Break it down for me," said Quinn.

Schuster's voice was as excited as a child's now. "I've been running on my own autopilot too much lately. The new thrusters allow us to get low without kicking up holy hell underneath us. Granted, that doesn't help in most situations because it's redistributed horizontally in a 360-degree radius—"

Gloom had joined them on the bridge and was next to Schuster, bent over the control panels.

"Which means instead of thrusting down, you're thrusting out," she finished for him. "It won't kick up debris and everything underneath us, but it'll shatter the glass in any buildings we fly past."

Schuster grinned. "But there *are* no tall buildings left in Rome, at least not ones that aren't already teetering, so we can set down wherever we want."

"Won't we be hangin' a big sign on FUBAR that says 'steal me'?" asked Ulysses. The others had gathered round the entrance to the bridge now.

"I'll bring her in up in the hill, so we only have to walk down to get to the city," said Schuster. Beside him, Gloom was already fiddling with the controls.

Quinn finally threw up his hands. "Just land us and don't make a big mess," he sighed, exasperated.

Chelsea flashed him a smile. "Maggott's already awake," she said. "That was the biggest potential danger. What's the worst that can happen now?"

~

THEY KIPPED down for the night in the cargo hold, crashing on emergency kit bedrolls from the supply locker. It was far from comfortable, but exhaustion made for an excellent sleep aid.

They lit out again at dawn the next morning. Maggott was still yawning as they made their way down the Capitolene Hill, past what was left of the ruins of the Forum. It was all essentially rubble now, which made for tough hiking for all of them.

"I never came t'Italy as a kid," he said. "Couldnae afford the trip. Wish I'd seen it before everythin' went t'shite."

"Me, too," said Quinn. The sun was slowly rising in the eastern sky, which meant a huge orange ball hung in the air behind them, illuminating their path as they walked.

"Chelsea sez this here's the Fielda Mars up ahead." Ulysses pointed directly ahead and down from them. "You Jarheads were moanin' over not seein' the real thang when we went past, well, there's yer consolation prize."

Maggott ignored him. "And this Foster Kenya fella? I wuz asleep yesterday while you were drawin' up yuir plans."

"I ain't totally clear on that m'self," said Ulysses.

Quinn kept his eyes on his feet as they traversed the rocks, trying to keep his ankles intact and not to think about all the history they were stepping on in the process.

"Neither am I," he said. "Apparently he's world famous, at least with some segments of the population."

"Y'mean the ones in the Towers?" asked Maggott.

"Exactly. We didn't have time for media in the war, even when we could get access to it, so none of us have ever heard of him. But Chelsea didn't spend all her time in war zones, so she had more opportunity to watch the network feeds—and the outlaw feeds, too."

"I thought all that social media shit was outlawed a long time ago," said Ulysses. "Like 'fore we was even born. Didn't it cause nuthin' but problems?"

"Depends on how you look at it, but yeah, that was the general gist of it. The governments took control of all the broadcast media and outlawed private news feeds on the network, so that private citizens weren't able to put their own content online anymore. People like us three never knew about any of that because, in the slums, we were lucky just to have access to the public archives. The online network was for Tower folks."

Quinn could hear Maggott's labored breathing, so he stopped to give him a quick break.

"Anyway, apparently Foster Kenya is this outlaw journalist who goes all over the world, digging into corruption and broadcasting what he discovers out over the network. He somehow bypasses the tech that bans everyone else and hijacks the wi-fi waves. People on the lower levels of the Towers eat it up, according to Chelsea. Sticking it to the man sells, I guess."

"Not enoughta pull 'em away from their CR terminals," Ulysses said bitterly. "Or to make 'em actually climb outta their Towers and walk around on the ground with the slumdogs. But I'm sure they all sit 'round at their cocktail parties and talk 'bout how horrible it all is, and that somebody oughta do sump'n."

"Aye." Maggott nodded. "S'always somebody else's job."

The others had stopped about a hundred meters ahead of them and were motioning for them to hurry up. Quinn raised a hand back in acknowledgment before they set out again.

"Now's not the time to judge mankind," he said. "Now's the time to get them to listen to us. And from what Gloom and Chelsea say, this guy Kenya is the best hope we have. So that's what I'm going to focus on."

"At least till the next time we're ambushed," Maggott grumbled.

Quinn and Ulysses shared a look, and both started to snicker. What else could they do? There was no arguing with what the man had said.

~

QUINN THOUGHT he'd been prepared for what they would find in the city proper, but as soon as they could make out the river through the haze, he knew it would be worse than he'd imagined.

Every building left standing was packed with throngs of people, crammed together without personal space and obviously malnourished. He saw that very few people even wore shoes, though the odd one was well-dressed. They were usually muscular young men and women, Rome's equivalent of the Southern Saints, the gangs that ostensibly looked after the people who couldn't protect themselves.

As they walked on the ancient cobblestones, Quinn found himself growing angrier with each step. Children were wailing openly, their poor parents too exhausted to care for them or even comfort them. There were plenty of vendors on the street, selling everything from food to bootleg CR experiences, just like in Vegas, but they were right next to people who were starving and yet offered them nothing. Meanwhile, bored-looking men and women in gaudy outfits filled every doorway, beckoning people to join them for some fun.

Chelsea and Gloom flanked him as he stopped to stare at what had once been the Pantheon but was now just another bombed-out makeshift shelter with broken columns littering the entryway.

"I know, it's unbelievable," said Chelsea. "It's like the city wallows in the horror. No Towers, no police, no militia."

"No hope," said Quinn.

Gloom scanned the area. "It's worse than what you can see here. There are people who come to Rome from all over the world, like it's some kind of Mecca for sickos with no moral compass, or who get off on suffering. There are vacation packages for people to hunt other humans through the city. And it's a haven for organized crime." She turned to Ulysses. "No offense."

He shrugged. "No skin offa *my* nose."

Quinn felt his stomach hitch. Chelsea simply nodded.

"I have no doubt that it's as bad as you say. It makes sense that your friend would use it as his home base. No one would ever chase him here."

"Why doesn't he report about *this?*" asked Quinn, sweeping a hand at the misery surrounding them. "This is a nightmare."

"You can ask him yourself," said Gloom, glancing at the monitor of her custom wrist unit. "He just pinged me. He's nearby."

"All right," said Chelsea, looking in a different direction. "I'll meet you back here in a few minutes."

Quinn frowned. "What are you up to?"

He followed her gaze to a small alcove, where a well-dressed man with fair, sunburnt skin and blond hair was handling bills and wristbands across a small wooden counter. Quinn suddenly understood what she meant to do.

"I'm coming with you," he protested.

"No, you're not." Chelsea grabbed Gloom by the arm. "You're going over there somewhere. *She's* coming with me."

Everything inside him wanted to argue, but he also realized that Gloom had been the one who saved all their lives less than thirty-six hours earlier, not to mention leading them here.

The girl offered him a resigned shrug as she trotted to catch up with Chelsea, until they were both walking toward the pink man with the money.

Quinn, Chelsea, Gloom and Ellie stepped off the street and into an old café that was relatively intact for the area, which meant that the walls were still holding up the ceiling. A fat man with sweat running down the back of his bald head worked a steamy machine of some sort to produce large cups of a frothy gray liquid that Quinn assumed was coffee. Under the machine was an open display case of baked goods that looked hard as stone.

"Keep that money out of sight," Quinn muttered to Chelsea.

"It's already in my pocket, Quinn," she said testily. "Where *should* I keep it, up my cooch?"

Gloom snorted a laugh and Quinn glowered. Ellie looked embarrassed for him.

"I apologize," he grumbled. "I'm used to giving orders."

"Not to me, you're not," said Chelsea. "Technically, this seventy grand is all mine, even if it *is* only one percent of what that ankle bracelet was worth."

"Not to mention more than I made in the last eight years combined," Ellie said quietly.

Gloom pointed to a table and the four sat down. It was rickety and wobbled, so when Chelsea arrived with coffee for them, it spilled into the saucers of every cup. But it was hot, and Quinn was surprised that it didn't actually taste all that bad.

"Heads up," Gloom whispered as a gangly man with a shaggy beard and an embroidered pillbox hat walked in and crossed to a table several meters away.

"Is that him?" Quinn asked.

"We'll see." Gloom tapped Ellie's leg. "It's your show."

Ellie flashed them a nervous look, and Quinn was glad Bishop wasn't there to see it. She made her way to the man's table and stood next to it. The man raised his head to look her in the face.

"Hat, beard," she said.

The man nodded. "Tall redhead."

With that, he stood and left. Ellie walked back to their table, bewildered.

"What happened?" she asked. "I said what you told me to say, and he answered the way you said he would."

"Which is why I'm here," said a male voice from behind her.

Ellie flinched, but managed to hold in the yelp that Quinn had expected to hear. He leaned over to see past her to a young man with ebony skin and long hair standing behind her, wearing a tattered button-down shirt and khaki jeans. His weather-beaten military-style boots looked like they'd logged many miles in their time.

"It's double encryption," Gloom said with a grin as she rose from the table. "We each used an agent to introduce ourselves. By having someone matching the description show up, we know that the message has been received without actually giving ourselves away. Once that step is over, we can trust that we are who we're supposed to be and not someone attempting an ambush."

Quinn raised an eyebrow. That was actually quite clever.

Gloom embraced the newcomer, who hugged her back.

"It's good to finally put a face to the name," said the man, who was obviously the Foster Kenya they'd been seeking.

"Wait, you two have never met before right now?" asked Quinn, confused.

Gloom motioned for the newcomer to sit with them. "It's quite possible to know someone without physically meeting them," she said in a tone that indicated she didn't think she should have to explain something so simple.

"So you're—" Chelsea started, but Kenya held up a hand.

"Please, call me Ben," he said with a warm smile. "I try not to use the other one in public, for obvious reasons."

Chelsea nodded. "Of course. We try to do the same, for the same reasons."

"Well, it's slightly different for us," said Quinn. "We have people trying to kill us."

"So do I," Ben said evenly. "And pretty soon I'll have even more, if what Gloom hinted to me is true. I'd say we should get out of here and go someplace where we can talk in private."

The others turned to Quinn, looking for the go-ahead, which made him feel a tiny bit better. He nodded, and they rose and headed for the street, Gloom and Ben taking point, chatting and laughing like old friends. For some reason he couldn't put his finger on, Quinn found himself envying them a little.

~

UNLIKE BOCEPHUS AND GLOOM, Ben's home was a bona fide dump. It was under the ruins of a Roman villa that sat at the base of one of the so-called Seven Hills. It had likely been excavated and carefully preserved for centuries before the Trilateral War, but now it was just another place to seek shelter. The faint ghost of burnt sienna on the wall might have been the remains of an ancient fresco, but could just as easily have been the fading remains of blood from one of a hundred battles during the war.

The space was open and all but empty, the dirt floor littered with debris. A trio of locked cabinets and a spring-loaded single cot sat beside a stainless steel box about the size and shape of an old steamer trunk from the days when people still travelled by boat.

The women sat side-by-side on the cot while the men took the floor. Chelsea had bought them a feast of greasy street food on the way to Ben's—with Quinn admonishing her to keep her money hidden, of course—and they were all dealing with the effects of the aftermath, including elevated blood sugar and the sleepiness that resulted from blood rushing from their brains to their bellies to help with digestion. And, at the moment, there was no one actively trying to kill them.

In other words, they felt truly relaxed for the first time in quite a while.

"I almost feel human again," Chelsea sighed.

Bishop cocked a thumb in Maggott's direction. "That's how Ursa Major here feels all the time: *almost* human."

Maggott responded by beaning him with the remains of a potato pancake, prompting a cackle from Ellie. Schuster, meanwhile, couldn't seem to take his eyes off of Gloom, and Ulysses appeared to be dozing. Quinn glanced at his wristband: 0900. They were about as rested as they could have hoped to be at that point. It was time to get down to business.

"So Ben," he said. "From what Gloom tells us, you're able to hack into the global network and broadcast directly to the public."

Ben nodded and pointed to the metal trunk in the corner of the room.

"That's my entire media empire right there: work station and broadcasting tech in one. It locks up tight when I don't need it, but opens automatically with my retinal scan. I can even take it with me. It's cutting edge."

"Looks like a box," Maggott observed.

"Looks can be deceiving," said Quinn. "Remember when that little Yandare almost broke your nose on Oberon One?"

Maggott scowled, but Ben leaned closer to Quinn, tenting his fingers under his chin.

"So it's true," he said softly. "To be honest, the skeptic in me was still taking this all with a grain of salt. But you really did come from space." He blinked. "Wait a minute, did you say you actually saw a *Yandare?*"

"Focus, Ben." Gloom sat down on the floor next to him. "You're trying to stop an alien invasion, not track down mythical assassins."

"Nothin' mythical 'bout Yandares," said Ulysses.

"A-bloody-men," Maggott agreed.

"Can we stick to the point?" Quinn snapped. "Yes, we are who we say we are and yes, we came from Oberon One."

"That much I'm sure of," he said. "I looked you up online after Gloom got in touch. It wasn't hard; your wanted posters are all over the network now, and they match the mug shots of the four men convicted of treason two years ago."

Quinn gave him a grim smile. "Lucky us. Now can we move on?

Just set us up in front of the camera and we can get to recording our story."

"It's not that simple. I said I believe you are who you say you are, but I need to have some sort of proof about the whole *Invasion of the Body Snatchers* thing before I put you out on the network."

"Invasion of the *what?*" Chelsea asked.

"Body Snatchers," said Gloom. "Super old movie on the archives about alien spores that took over human brains."

"I need evidence," said Ben. "Every time I hack into the network to broadcast something, I'm putting myself at risk of being captured or killed, so I don't just do it on someone else's say-so. Do I believe that you all encountered something that's driving you to do what you're doing? Absolutely. But that's not enough."

Schuster cleared his throat. "We've got a Raft up in the hills that has some serious upgrades I could show you, if that helps."

Ben shook his head. "That's just proof of technology. As far as I or any of my audience knows, that could just be some of the experimental stuff out of the Prometheus lab in Antarctica."

"You know about that?" asked Quinn. The rumors of a Prometheus black site had circled in the military for years during the war, but no one had ever found proof—at least, not that he knew of.

"You *have* been out of the loop," said Chelsea. "Foster Kenya broke that story before I left Earth for Uranus last year."

Ben grinned. "Just about froze my ass off, but I was pretty proud of that one."

"What're y'all talkin''bout?" asked Ulysses. "What's Prometheus?"

"A war profiteer." Quinn peered at their new potential ally. "How did you find out about Antarctica? Who did you talk to?"

Ben grinned. "A good journalist never reveals his sources. Suffice to say that there are people in high places who get off on giving away secrets. And there are even some who want to change things for the better. Not a hell of a lot of them, granted, but a few."

"How did you convince your viewers that Prometheus was real?"

"I broke into their Antarctic base and got footage of their testing labs."

Whoa. "That's impressive," said Quinn.

"It's not easy changing the world." Ben shrugged. "Seventy percent of the population is just trying to live to see another sunrise, while thirty percent are too busy living out their fantasies in cortical reality to give a shit. That leaves the statistically insignificant fraction of a percent who are the ones profiting from the way the world is, and they'll do anything to keep the boat from rocking. What I'm trying to do is reach as many as I can who are on the fringes of that upper strata and get them to think."

"I'm one of those," said Chelsea, holding up a hand like a schoolgirl. "I was a huge fan before I left for Uranus. You really do an amazing job of exposing the dirty secrets of modern society."

"Yeah?" asked Ulysses. "So what'dja do about what you found out, Doc? Besides cluck yer tongue, I mean."

Her eyes flashed. "I served in the war," she said icily. "Did you?"

"Every day's a war where I come from, lady."

"Stow it, you two," Quinn said wearily. "So what do you need from us, Ben?"

"An interview, to start."

Ben got up and placed his face against the scanner of the metal trunk so that it could read his retinal signature. A moment later, servos opened up a miniature work station, complete with extending legs, while three flexible screens unrolled. He motioned for Quinn to sit while he set up a spherical holocamera on the floor.

Quinn sat where he was told. "Where do you want me to start?"

"At the beginning. State your name first, please."

"All right," Quinn sighed and looked into the camera. "My name is Napoleon Quinn, formerly of the United Free Territories Marines. A little over two years ago, my team and I were in Sao Paulo, trying to stop a weapon that had been set by a terrorist group called the Children of Saul..."

~

IT WAS the second time he'd told the story in as many days, but it didn't make it any easier for him to believe. For his part, Ben didn't interrupt him once. In fact, he hadn't said a single word since he'd turned on the camera.

When Quinn finished, Ben sat in silence for a minute or longer, staring at his hands. Then he looked over at Dev Schuster with wide eyes.

"So you've got one?" he asked. "An alien, I mean. In your brain."

Schuster squirmed a bit. "That's not exactly how I like to think of it, but yeah, I suppose that's one way to put it."

"Do you have any *tangible* proof?"

"I can't call it up like a commlink, if that's what you mean."

Ben shook his head. "Yeah, I don't really know what I was thinking there. See, that's the biggest problem with this. Without actual little green men to look at, the public will think it's just a hoax."

"But they trust you," said Quinn.

"No, they trust the *facts* that I bring them. The evidence. Without that, they're not going to believe me, especially about something like this. In fact, I have to admit that even *I'm* still skeptical; I mean, I believe that *you* all believe it, but I'd rather have the smoking gun in my hand."

Bishop, who had taken Gloom's seat next to Ellie on the cot, looked deep in thought. Quinn had learned to trust his friend's insight over the years; where he himself tended to shoot first and ask questions later, Bishop was often his sober second thought. It's why they'd worked so well together for so many years.

"What's on your mind, Geordie?"

"I was just thinking that what Ben says makes sense," said Bishop. "No one in their right mind would believe our story."

"Excuse me?" Gloom said indignantly.

Bishop ignored her. "And maybe we're wasting our time even trying to convince them."

Quinn frowned. "That's not how Marines talk, Lieutenant."

"I'm not saying give up, Lee. You know me better than that."

"So do I." Ellie took his hand. "So what *are* you saying?"

"I'm saying maybe we should just cut the Gordian knot and go for broke. Ben just said he's got connections with Prometheus, or whatever's left of it. Maybe we can find some of their weapons, load them up on FUBAR and head back to Oberon One. As far as we know, there's been no official response to the breakout, right?"

They all looked at each other and shrugged.

"I haven't seen anything on the network other than the fact that you four escaped," said Gloom. "No details at all."

"So there's nothing to stop us from heading back and taking on Kergan and his drones ourselves. Even if it means killing every last one of them, we'll have stopped them."

Quinn thought about it for a few moments before heaving a sigh.

"I wish it were that easy," he said. "I'd love a head-on fight. It's programmed into us to do things that way. But there's a big problem with that plan."

"Why?" asked Maggott. "I think it's fookin' genius. I'd happily kill Kergan with m'bare hands."

"Get in line," said Ulysses.

Chelsea stood up and stretched her legs, walking toward the far wall. "It's because the stakes are too high," she said. "Because if we lose that battle, it's over. It may come to that eventually, but before it does, we need to get everyone on Earth behind this if we can have a hope of beating whatever's coming through that wormhole."

"We have no idea how much we don't know," said Quinn. "How long will it take to create the wormhole? We don't know. How many troops will be coming through when it does open up? We don't know. What kind of weapons will it take to defeat them? Until Schuster can practice how to call up the information that was dumped in his brain, we just don't know."

"Man," said Ulysses. "Seems like the only thing you *do* know is how to piss on our campfire, Quinn."

"But he's right," said Gloom. "United, at least, with billions of people behind us, the Earth might have a shot. But a bunch of misfit Marines and a souped-up spaceship against an invading alien army?"

"Hey," Schuster said indignantly. "I'll have you know these misfit

Marines managed to fight their way out of prison, steal a spaceship, beat a bunch of aliens and make it back to Earth."

"Y'ain't all Marines, neither," said Ulysses. "Right, Doc?"

"Damn straight."

Quinn jammed the heels of his palms into his eyes and watched the kaleidoscope of colors go off behind his eyes. They had travelled halfway around the world, but he didn't feel any closer to having a plan than he did when they were first flanked by those ships when they arrived.

Then a thought hit him like a hammer between the eyes.

"Ship," he breathed. "We did a hell of a lot in that ship, even before we left Oberon."

An instant later, Schuster's dark eyes almost popped out of his head.

"Holy shit," he said. "I can't believe I didn't think of it before now. The ship! Sloane and his people were with us in the ship!"

Gloom looked back and forth between the two men. "What are you talking about? What good is the ship?"

Quinn felt a grin spread across his face, and saw the same happening on Schuster's.

"The ship will have records!" Schuster crowed. "Rafts automatically record all the feeds from the sensors and cameras, including the ones inside! All the audio over the radios! Everything!"

Bishop looked thunderstruck. "You mean—"

"I mean we've got the evidence you're looking for, Ben." Quinn clapped the young man on the shoulder. "In living, breathing holographic video. All we have to do is get it out of the ship's data banks."

Gloom sat back and crossed her arms over her chest. The look on her face suggested she was impressed, but was trying not to let it show.

"Settle down," she said, looking at Schuster. "I would have figured it out eventually, too."

His grin widened as he gave her a patronizing nod. "Of course you would have."

"Don't push it," she said, but there was a hint of humor in her voice.

"Well?" Quinn asked.

Ben lifted his hands, palms up. "I can't think of better evidence than a ship's records. Let's get them and get it on the network."

"Oorah!" shouted Maggott. "We're finally doon somethin'!"

Quinn stood up to head for the door, but he didn't make it ten steps before the wall suddenly exploded inward, knocking him to the floor and burying him in chunks of broken concrete. Somewhere in the room, a woman was screaming.

18

Quinn's eardrums were numb from the blast, but he could still hear enough to know that the screaming had stopped and had been replaced with yelling.

He struggled onto all fours. Chunks of concrete slid from his back, taking some flesh with them, but as far as he could tell, no bones were broken. In front of him, shadows moved around the room in the cloud of dust that had been created when the wall blasted inward. He tried to focus, to remember the positions of everyone in the room: he, Ulysses and Ben nearest the wall, Maggott and Schuster also close, Bishop and Ellie in the middle of the room, Gloom and Chelsea farthest from the blast.

He could make out shapes moving on the other side of the room through the cloud of concrete dust kicked up by the exploding wall. That's where the noise was coming from; commotion of some sort. More dust shadows rose slowly around him, but Quinn couldn't wait for them to get to their feet. He had to assess the situation and act *now*.

His legs weren't cooperating, though, and he stumbled forward instead of sprinting like he was trying to do. But he managed to cross the room and get to the other side of the dust cloud just in time to see a group of silhouettes racing up the ancient stairs that had led them down to Ben's apartment. Something was flailing in the mass of shadows, and that was the source of the noise. Finally, a few seconds too late, he was able to think clearly enough to understand: someone was kidnapping Chelsea.

"Jarheads!" he croaked. His voice sounded, and felt, like it was full of broken glass.

Quinn felt a hand on his shoulder and turned to see Bishop, struggling to stand. Ellie was on the floor, rubbing her head, an Gloom was nearby with her hand propped against the stair wall, coughing. Quinn could already feel his hearing starting to return as Bishop shouted in his face, "They got Chelsea!"

"I know." Quinn turned back to face the area where the wall had been. The dust had cleared enough that he could make out the rest of the men, all staggering but on their feet. He wasn't overly concerned about his men and Ulysses; it was Ben who was the wild card here.

He needn't have worried. Ben was already on the move toward his equipment. Under other circumstances, Quinn might have been furious, but he realized how important it was to their future that the tech be able to do what it needed to do.

"Jarheads topside!" he barked. "They've got Chelsea!"

Schuster and Maggott were at his and Bishop's side in a second. Quinn looked to Ulysses, whose scalp was covered in cuts and abrasions that trickled blood down into his eyes.

"Protect the civilians," he said. "We're going after the doc."

Ulysses nodded, wiping at his face with his sleeve. Quinn clapped him on the shoulder and made for the stairs, his men on his heels. He heard Ellie call after Bishop to be careful as they headed into the cramped stairwell and up the flight that would lead them to ground level.

They emerged into the open-air part of the villa and saw people scattering in the distance, obviously trying to get away from whatever had caused the blast, and not wanting to get involved with the people who had just come out of the stairs carrying a struggling, shouting woman.

Speaking of that, Quinn couldn't hear Chelsea any longer now that they were above ground. He tried not to think about what that might mean, focusing instead on the fact that she was of no value to them dead or injured.

"Orders, sir?" Maggott panted. He was hunched over, hands on his knees. Schuster was shaking his head to clear it, while Bishop, who appeared the least affected by the blast, scanned the street around them. They were close to a number of narrow side streets.

"Suggestions?" Quinn asked.

A young woman a dozen yards away pointed toward an alley that ran parallel along the wider street that they had taken to get to Ben's. She looked around furtively as she did so, obviously fearing reprisal if someone caught her giving them any information. Quinn nodded his thanks and they made their way into the alley, jogging as fast as their legs could manage under the circumstances.

"How'd the bastards set off that charge from outside?" Maggott huffed. "It's a fookin' basement!"

"There are all sorts of tunnels under the structures in this city," said Schuster. His eyes still didn't look completely focused. "There must have been one next to that wall."

"It was sonic," said Bishop. "At least, that's how it felt when it hit. You guys probably only noticed the concrete blasting into you."

"Just a wee bit," Maggott groaned, rubbing at his lower back.

They rounded a corner and emerged into a crowded piazza, where people were shouting and making a commotion about twenty meters ahead. Quinn felt his heart leap in his chest as he heard someone yell: "Yo! Put her down, asshole!" in what Quinn would have sworn was a Long Island accent.

A few more seconds of weaving through the crowd of people and Quinn was close enough to see what was happening. Four men in long wool cloaks were trying to push their way into the crumbling entrance to a building, but a well-dressed man pushed the lead one back every time they tried to move forward.

He caught sight of Chelsea, lying over the shoulder of one of the cloaked men, her eyes closed. *She's unconscious,* he told himself forcefully. *That's all.*

He pointed the others toward what he was seeing. "Maggott," he said. "Make a path."

The big man nodded and charged forward into the throng as Quinn and the others followed in his wake. A few people shouted complaints as they were shoved unceremoniously out of the way, but the majority seemed to be more than happy to move and avoid whatever was going on.

Before they could reach the door, Quinn saw that the guy who had been trying to bar them from entering was now lying on the sidewalk with blood streaming down his face. The quartet were inside the building and moving up a flight of stairs, which meant they would have the high ground.

Of course they will, Quinn sighed inwardly. *When is anything ever easy?*

The crowd had thinned considerably by the time they got to the entrance on the sidewalk. Apparently a bloody local on the ground was even more incentive to mind one's own business than an unconscious woman draped over a sinister-looking guy's shoulder.

Quinn knelt next to the man. He looked to be in his twenties, with dark hair and olive skin under the blood pouring from his nose. His frame was solid under his expensive clothes, which confirmed that he was likely a member of a gang—an American one, judging by his accent. Quinn looked up at the Jarheads and gave them a wink, which meant to follow his lead.

"You fuckin' kidding me?" he snapped to the man on the sidewalk. "How'd you let them in? Can't you do anything right?"

The guy blinked at him. "Who the fuck are you? I don't answer to you! Besides, those cyber pukes had me outnumbered!"

"Tell it to your boss, punk!" Quinn pointed to Maggott. "Give Mookie here your weapons and let the men handle it."

The guy glared hard at Maggott, as if recognizing him. He opened his mouth to protest, but appeared to think better of it when Maggott started reaching for him.

"Fine, whatever!" he yelped.

He reached into his jacket and withdrew what looked to Quinn like a cheap machine pistol, not unlike the Russian ones the Jarheads had used on their mission in Astana two years earlier. Quinn snatched it impatiently.

"Get home to your mama," he said, checking the pistol. Fully loaded, in good shape. "Maybe we won't tell anyone we saw you here."

The guy looked ready to argue, but Bishop slapped him in the back of the head before he could say anything.

"Did he stutter? Get the fuck gone!"

With one final look of reproach, the man began to swagger defiantly up the narrow street, but a couple of quick steps in his direction from Maggott were enough to make him quickly double his pace and start to jog instead.

"Holy shit," said Schuster, gaping at the pistol. "Are we actually *armed*? When was the last time that happened?"

"Too long," Quinn said with a grim smile. He motioned for them to take formation and move into the building's lobby. It was dark, so he led them to get their backs against the wall and face the stairwell.

"What do you think he meant by 'cyber pukes'?" asked Bishop.

Quinn took a quick scan of the building. "Wish I knew. This place is six stories, easily several hundred years old. Probably a labyrinth of small rooms and narrow hallways. Far from ideal fighting conditions, especially against an unknown opponent."

"Especially with their resources," said Schuster.

"What do you mean?"

"Well, for one thing, they had a sonic charge to take out that wall. For another, they were headed down the stairs the second that charge went off. Even if they had followed us to Ben's without us seeing them, they must have had thermal imaging tech at the very least, maybe even something more advanced, to know where we all were in the room."

Bishop nodded. "I see what you're saying. Otherwise they ran the risk of hurting or even killing Chelsea with the blast."

"Why the black bed sheets?" asked Maggott.

Quinn brandished the pistol. "Let's shoot one and ask him."

He took point and stalked up the stairs, the others following in formation to keep an eye all around them as they moved. At the first floor, Quinn ducked his head around the corner for a quick recon, ready to fire at anything that moved. He could hear commotion from inside the rooms, but apparently the people who lived there knew better than to stick their heads out when dangerous people were around. He was glad for that; the last thing he wanted was to get into a firefight with civilians in the crossfire. It was bad enough as it was with Chelsea as a human shield now, which reminded him to switch the pistol to single-shot action.

Then he heard another scream coming from above them, and he almost accidentally squeezed off a round. The others sidled up to him in the stairwell landing, backs to the wall.

"That was Chelsea," Quinn hissed, his heart galloping.

"Aye," Maggott whispered back. "But did ye hear it? She dinnae sound scared."

"I agree," said Bishop. "She sounded mad."

At that moment, someone came around the corner and surprised the hell out of them.

Chelsea watched the man stumble backward, having taken the full brunt of her kick square in the groin, and trip over a moldering old hassock in the middle of the floor. He landed hard on his back with a metallic clank.

Wait a minute: Clank?

The other three were trying to surround her, all of them still wrapped in those stupid wool robes, but none had approached her except the one she'd just kicked. That meant one thing: they were after a reward, and they wouldn't hurt her. She, on the other hand, could do whatever she wanted to them.

She could see their faces—all men, all pale—but their bodies were hidden by the baggy black clothes. Without serious auto-cooling tech, she couldn't imagine how they could possibly not have heat exhaustion, given the sweltering temperature of the day.

"What the hell did you hit me with?" she growled.

"Calm down!" the one in the middle pleaded. "We don't want to hurt you!"

"Answer my question! How did you knock me out and then revive me like you did?"

"Don't tell her," the one to her left warned. "Oh, man, this shouldn't be so frigging hard!"

"Shut up!" said the middle man. "Look, lady, it was just infrasonics, okay? We weren't gonna hurt you!"

"Tell your dad we didn't hurt you!" the one to her right blurted.

Chelsea decided she was tired of the discussion and rushed the one to her right. She closed the distance in two steps and stamped her heel into the inside of his right thigh, driving him to the floor. At the same time, she snared the hood of his cloak and yanked it off of him, tossing it to the floor behind her.

What she saw made the breath catch in her throat.

"Ah, shit," the middle man muttered. "Why'd you have to do that, lady? Now everything's gonna be so much worse."

~

Schuster glared at Gloom, his mouth working like a fish on dry land. Quinn and the other three took deep breaths trying to still their pounding hearts.

"What the hell is the matter with you?" Schuster hissed. "Don't sneak up on people like that!"

"I told you to stay with Ben!" Quinn whispered fiercely. "If you're going to work with us, you follow my orders."

Gloom raised a delicately tapered middle finger in his direction.

"You'd be dead if it weren't for me in Vegas," she said evenly. "Also, that's no way to talk to someone who brought you guns."

She unshouldered her pack and opened the top, withdrawing a

Kelly AutoMAG for each of them. They were standard issue for military in two of the three factions of the war, and the Jarheads were familiar with them.

"Courtesy of Ben," she said. "The man's nothing if not resourceful."

"What about you?" Schuster asked.

Gloom grinned and pulled out the box that Quinn recognized from the night at the Golden Nugget.

"I got this."

"What good is that?" he snapped.

"Look, I saw these guys as they grabbed Chelsea. They're dressed in black, they had some sort of tech that knocked her out, they had sonic charges to blow in the wall and some sort of sensors to read the inside of the room."

"I already said that," Schuster griped.

Gloom ignored him. "I'll bet every source code in my system that these are the same guys from Vegas."

Bishop cocked his head. "She's got a point, Lee."

"How'd they know we were in Rome?" asked Maggott.

She threw up her hands. "Fine, you guys sit here and think about that, I'll go rescue Chelsea."

"All right, all right, point taken," said Quinn. "But you told me the other night that your tech wouldn't work a second time."

"The same trick, no, but that was a generic virus that would have shut down just about anything for a few minutes. I fiddled with the box on the flight over so that it should be able to read the suits' broadcast frequency once we get close enough. If I find the frequency, I might be able to plant a more specific virus through it."

"What if it's a closed system?" Schuster asked defiantly.

She gave him a cool look. "Then I guess it'll be up to you to save *my* ass this time."

Quinn had to give the girl credit—she had guts to spare. Suddenly another shout came from upstairs, except this time the voice was male.

"Move," he hissed, raising his hand and motioning them forward to the stairs. They followed as one, and on a fundamental level, he felt better than he had in years. They were armed, they were in formation, they were stalking an enemy combatant.

"Feels like home," Maggott sighed, as if reading his mind.

The shouting got louder as they reached the second-floor landing. Quinn held up a fist for them to stop at the entrance to the long, narrow hallway. A hole in the wall at the far end where he assumed a window once stood provided the only light.

He motioned for Gloom to move into the middle of the pack, with himself and Maggott taking the front and Bishop and Schuster bringing up the rear. He didn't give her a chance to protest, he just started moving forward toward the noise.

"Don't!" another male voice cried from inside a room just as Quinn reached the door. Every instinct in him wanted to kick it in and start firing, but he turned back to Gloom.

"Are you reading them?"

She looked confused. "I don't understand—there's nothing showing up except the public wi-fi."

"What does that mean?" he asked, rolling his hand for her to get to the point.

"Closed system," Schuster said smugly.

"It means that there are no signals coming in or going out," she said. "That could mean a closed system, but there's no way they could have changed the fundamental method of operation on their smart suits between Vegas and here."

"Different suits?" Bishop offered.

"Does it matter?" asked Maggott. "I'm bettin' their heeds explode just the same when a bullet comes out the back."

Gloom glared at him. "You can't interrogate a dead man."

"Yeah, and dead men can't kill you," said Quinn. "But she's right; we have to keep it in our pants for Chelsea's sake. If you're going to take a shot, you damn well better hit exactly what you're aiming at. Stay low, go for body mass first."

"We know the drill," said Bishop.

"Says the man whose girl is safely out of the line of fire."

As soon as the words were out of his mouth, Quinn wished he could take them back, and not just because it had been a cheap shot at Geordie. What was he saying about Chelsea? Didn't matter. He waved his hand and stepped closer to the door. The others fell in behind him and waited for his signal to move.

Three seconds later, he gave it and kicked the flimsy door off its hinges with a single stomp of his boot. What he saw when he rushed into the apartment left him speechless. Given the events of the past six weeks, that was saying something.

19

Chelsea stood in a fighting stance, squared off against three men in cloaks while a fourth was on the floor, looking up at her. It was that one who had caught Quinn's immediate attention: the man's right arm looked more like a robotic appendage than something that belonged on a human. His torso was also abnormally large under his dark sweater, which could only mean one thing.

"Cyborgs!" Quinn barked as he took position in the center of the room, levelling his pistol at the one on the floor. The other Jarheads followed quickly, each aiming at one of the other three who were still standing.

"Ah, shit!" the guy in the middle cried. "Don't shoot! We don't want a fight!"

Quinn advanced on the middle one, keeping his pistol between the bald man's eyes. He'd only met a handful of cyborgs in his life and he'd never trusted one.

"You may not want a fight, but you got one." He raised his chin in Chelsea's direction. "She comes with us, period."

"Look, maybe we can figure something out," said the middle man. His left arm was similar to the man on the floor's, bulky and large under his clothing. "We take her for the reward, we let you go and don't tell anyone we saw you."

"Wow, how could we pass up a deal like that?" said Bishop, adjusting the grip on his pistol, which was aimed at the man to Chelsea's left.

Out of the corner of his eye, Quinn saw Gloom kneel next to the man on the floor, oblivious to what was going on around her, her eyes on her device.

"That's why I didn't pick anything up," she muttered. "It's not just a closed system, it's an *old* closed system. Might as well be trying to read hieroglyphics—"

Schuster took his eyes off his man for one second and turned to Gloom, but before he could warn her, the guy on the floor was moving. His robotic arm shot out a metal cable that snaked around her throat and tightened instantly. Her eyes were suddenly very wide and very much paying attention to the situation.

Quinn's stomach dropped as he realized they'd just lost their advantage. His mind raced through options.

The cyborg on the floor had stood up, pulling Gloom along with him. She clutched at the cable around her throat; it wasn't tight enough to hurt her or cut off her air, but it was more than tight enough to make her eyes blaze with fury.

"Jesus," the middle one groaned. "We just wanted the reward, we didn't want to kill anybody."

"So ye blew up a fookin' *wall* on us?" Maggott barked.

"We had to get her *somehow*," said the man to Chelsea's right, who was now firmly in Schuster's sights again. "That was the only way we could make sure to incapacitate without harming her."

"How did you find out about us?" Quinn demanded.

The men looked at each other, as if it was the stupidest question they ever heard.

"Are you fucking joking?" asked the middle one. "You're the most wanted people on the planet! There's ten million UFT credits to whoever brings in Chelsea Bloom unharmed. Another million if we bring you four's heads in. But we won't do that if you just let us go."

Quinn took a deep breath. At least now they knew that they were no longer ahead of the game, so they could plan accordingly, and hopefully not just their own funerals.

"Unfortunately," he said, "we've grown kind of attached to Dr. Bloom, so the answer's no."

Chelsea glowered. "First of all, it's me making the rules here, and second, how many times do I have to tell you I'm not a doctor!"

"Seriously?" Quinn gaped. "That's what you focus on?"

There was a whirring noise as the man holding Gloom lifted his robotic arm a touch. With that, the girl's face reddened immediately and the defiance in her eyes quickly dissipated. She dropped her device to the floor, where it landed with a heavy clack.

"Remember what's at stake here," said the cyborg.

Quinn acted without thinking, shuffling forward and surprising the middle man, until the tip of his pistol's muzzle was touching the skin between the cyborg's eyes. Up close, Quinn could smell the raging stink of fear sweat on him.

"I'd advise you to do the same," he said coldly.

He was ready for anything. Anything except what happened next, anyway. Quick as a snake, Chelsea reached out and grabbed an empty bottle that was lying on the plaster mantel of the ancient fireplace next to her and smashed it into a jagged edge. An instant later, the business end was at her own throat.

"Stand down!" she hollered. "Everyone just calm the fuck down!"

Yup, that was the voice we heard earlier, Quinn thought stupidly, still trying to process what was happening. At least everyone was taking a beat to listen to her. For now, anyway.

"We've got a Mexican standoff here," she said to the man in the middle. "You've got one of us, they've got you in their sights and the golden goose here is ready to slit her own throat. If anyone does literally anything here, things are going to get ugly."

"Jesus," the middle man groaned. It was almost a whine. "I should've known it was too good to be true."

"Shut up!" said the one who had Gloom.

"Look, I get it," said Chelsea, keeping the bottle near her throat. "Ten million credits is a lot of money."

"Especially when you have nothing," said the middle man. "Rome is the worst place on Earth. There's nothing here; no jobs, no money, no hope. Nothing."

"Then why do you live here?" asked Quinn. "No one's holding a gun to your head—" He stopped, realizing too late how stupid that sounded when his muzzle was literally between the man's eyes. "What I mean is, you could move if you wanted to. Find jobs."

The man to Chelsea's right barked a harsh laugh. "Right! Where we gonna go? Cyborgs are illegal."

"I thought you were granted amnesty after the war," said Chelsea.

Quinn's mind flashed back to those days. Cyborgs were technically illegal, but they were routinely used as mercenaries during war, starting back in the 2070s. People in the direst of circumstances would volunteer to undergo the procedure to be grafted to robotics as a last-ditch effort to make something of themselves, but in most cases, it didn't work out that way. Even now, thirty years after they first appeared, cyborgs were still looked down on by the vast majority of people, including the slumdogs. It was a way to make them feel better about their own lot. *My life is shit,* the saying went, *but at least I'm not a cyborg.*

"You thought wrong," said the middle man. "Yeah, police and militia don't actively hunt us down, but no one is willing to hire us. And we spend almost everything we can scrounge on keeping ourselves charged. Otherwise we wouldn't even be able to move."

"Yuir breakin' m'heart, princess," Maggott growled.

"That's enough, Maggott," said Chelsea. The fire had gone out of her voice and her eyes now. In the middle of the room, Quinn could see Gloom breathing easier as the cable around her neck eased off slightly. Tensions were going down. That was a good thing, right?

"Your images have been up around the city since yesterday," said the one in the middle. "When we saw the big one in the piazza this morning, we couldn't believe our luck. It was like winning the lottery."

Maggott's face went red.

"How did you find out about Chelsea?" asked Quinn.

The cyborg's brows rose, as if the answer should be obvious. "Everybody's talking about it. The whole city is after her. That guy we were fighting with outside was trying to take her away from us."

Quinn scowled. That's why the guy had looked like he recognized Maggott: he'd seen the wanted posters. And they'd let him go, which meant he'd probably told others they were there. They had to get Ben and get the hell out of Rome ASAP. There was no worse place for them to be right now.

But how? He racked his brain for a solution, but, as usual, Chelsea surprised him again.

"I've got a proposal," she said. "Even if by some miracle you do manage to get me out of here, which is a big if, some or all of you are going to end up injured or dead."

"We can say the same about you," said the man who had Gloom. She was beginning to look furious again.

"So here's the deal," said Chelsea. "I give you fifty thousand euros, cash, right now, and everyone walks away."

Everyone in the room exchanged looks. Quinn had to admit it was a better idea than he would have come up with. Every plan that had run through his head involved fighting their way out.

"How do we know you won't just shoot the second I let her go?" asked the one with the cable arm.

"You don't," said Chelsea. "But then again, we don't know you won't attack the second you've got the money in your hands, either. I guess we have to just trust each other."

The middle man glanced at the two others flanking him. "Fifty grand is a fortune, boys."

"Yeah," said the one to the right. "But this wasn't just about money. If people like us were the ones to bring her back to Oscar Bloom—"

"He'd probably have you arrested on the spot," said Chelsea. "Trust me, I've known him longer than you. If you thought you'd somehow strike a blow for cyborg rights, you're sorely mistaken."

The men looked at each other one last time and nodded. A second later, the thick cable slithered off of Gloom's throat. She rubbed her hand along the skin there and shot the cyborg a look that could curdle milk, but she didn't say anything. Instead, she crouched and picked up her device off the floor.

The Jarheads lowered their pistols slowly, until everyone was just standing there, looking suspicious.

"Money?" the middle guy asked, waving his human hand.

Chelsea withdrew the stack of bills from her pocket and handed it to him. The guy immediately stuffed it into his cloak.

"Not going to count it?" Quinn asked.

"Money's money," the man said, and Quinn thought his voice sounded suddenly morose. Defeated. "We take what we can get."

With that, Quinn and his people watched the quartet turn to the door and file out of the apartment. He was amazed to find himself actually feeling sorry for them.

"That was brilliant," said Gloom.

Quinn nodded. "I agree. Way to think outside the box."

"One of us has to," Chelsea sighed, dropping the remains of the bottle onto the floor, where it shattered. "I sometimes think you four *live* in the frigging box."

The men passed a look amongst themselves as they headed into the hallway. The cyborgs were gone, so the six of them made their way to the stairwell and back down to the main floor entry. Quinn's stomach dropped when he saw what was outside the openings where the doors had once been: a crowd of people on the cobblestone street outside the building, looking directly at them and pointing.

"There they are!" yelled a familiar voice. It was the guy they'd sent on their way earlier, and he was surrounded by a half-dozen similarly tough-looking young men, plus a couple of women.

Quinn stepped in front of Chelsea and Gloom and pulled the pistol from the back of his pants. His men did the same, creating a perimeter around the women and aiming outwards at the throng of people. They might not make it out of this, but damned if they weren't going to take as many as they could with them.

Quinn flexed his finger on the trigger as the guy and his companions made their way toward them, but let it go again as the first one's head was knocked sideways by a crackling ball of blue light. He heard the sound an instant later as more light rained down on the crowd, sending them scattering for cover.

He looked to his right just as a cube van skidded to a stop in front of the entrance. On the van's roof, a man with copper-colored skin was in a sniper's crouch with a more streamlined version of the shock rifles he'd seen so many times in prison. This one looked, in fact, a lot like the one the man with Quinn's face had used in the casino two nights earlier.

"Somebody call for the cavalry?" Ulysses hooted, squeezing off a few more rounds into the crowd.

Ellie burst through the doors in the back of the van and hustled them all inside. Ben was in the driver's seat, watching the carnage going on around them with eyes wide.

"Go!" Quinn cried as soon as the door was closed behind them and he saw Ulysses leap into the passenger seat. "Make for Capitolene Hill! The whole fucking city is after us!"

The van careened into the street, forcing people to scramble out of the way. Ben drove the narrow, crowded streets like an old pro, forcing them to grab hold of their seats to keep from being tossed around the back of the van by every sharp turn. After ten minutes or so, Quinn looked out the window to see that that crowd had thinned. If anyone was after them, they were far behind by now unless they were in the air.

"My heart's going a mile a minute," Ben said as he stepped on the accelerator in the clearing they had walked through earlier in the day that led to the base of Capitolene Hill. "Is it always like this for you people?"

"Now you see why I threw in with them," said Gloom, a huge grin on her face.

Ulysses pointed Ben in the direction of where they'd landed FUBAR, near the ruins of a bombed-out fountain. He had to warn

Ben to look for the edges of the holographic camo before the van drove directly into the side of the ship.

They filed out almost as one, Bishop with his arm tightly wrapped around Ellie. Schuster shut down the hologram and FUBAR reappeared as if by magic.

Ben stared at it, his mouth hanging open.

"Seriously? You came all the way from Uranus in *this?*"

The group stood waiting for the rear door to complete its drop, and Quinn smiled.

"In a lot of ways, FUBAR's more of a home than anything we've known for years," he said.

"Her name is FUBAR?" Ben grinned. "I'd like to hear the story behind that."

"So would I," said a voice from inside the ship, and Quinn's guts froze.

He looked up into the ship's cargo hold and saw his own face looking back at him, along with three other men whose faces were covered by the helmets of their smart suits.

"Come aboard," he said with a grin. "You can tell us the story and we'll all have some fun. I really should introduce myself, since we keep meeting like this. You can call me Zero."

20

The passage of time had never bothered the entity that was now part of Ervin "Butch" Kergan before. Time was, after all, of no consequence, as Kevin Sloane had been so fond of saying. Their race was sentient thought, existing in its native form as something independent of the space-time continuum. Of course, in order to propagate the species, they had to manifest in this universe, but for the most part, it was simply a part of the process. It meant nothing.

Then they had gotten involved with these humans, and suddenly everything had changed.

The entities that had become Kergan and Sloane had emerged after the meteorite strikes on the moon Oberon and joined with their vessels on the moon's surface. That was standard operating procedure. But over the next two weeks, they had begun to experience their hosts' emotions in ways that their species never had in the past. That had led to all sorts of unpleasantness, and now Kergan was alone on the Oberon One space station. He was surrounded by more than a hundred humans, yes, but they were all controlled by his own mind. Essentially, they were just reflections of him.

In short, he was bored out of his skull, which made him appreciate his new friend even more.

He was in his office, which had previously belonged to Warden Sean Farrell, when the commlink indicator sounded. He spent most of his time in the office these days; it had its own toilet for his vessel's annoying bodily functions, and the gravity was consistent. Anything else he needed was brought to him by his many drones.

Kergan grinned widely as he answered the call and the holographic face of Dr. Toomey filled the sphere in front of him.

"Hello, Doctor," he chimed brightly. "So good to see you again."

"And you, Officer," said the man, though he didn't seem to mean it. His face was always so grim. "I thought it best to keep you apprised of the situation here on Earth. My agents have just made contact with the Bloom woman, as well as Quinn and his men. Also the inmate who escaped with them, and three other people I don't know."

"Is that so?" Kergan leaned forward in his seat. He found this intriguing indeed. "And what will your men do with them now, Doctor?"

"Return the woman to her father and kill the others, as you requested."

"Excellent," said Kergan. In truth, he would have much rather Dr. Toomey brought those people back to Oberon One, but he realized they were much too dangerous alive.

"This is going quite well," said the doctor. "By recovering Ms. Bloom, I'll ingratiate myself that much more with Oscar Bloom."

Kergan was starting to get bored again. "I'm very happy for you, Doctor. But how, exactly, will this impact *our* situation?"

Toomey blinked. "I thought that would be obvious. By recovering the modified ship stolen by Quinn and his men, I'll be able to reach Oberon One much more quickly than by conventional means."

"Ah!" Kergan grinned. "And you'll bring the supplies with you! How wonderful!"

The two men had played an infinitely fun game of cat-and-mouse over the past three days, where Kergan hinted to Toomey that there was much more to be learned on Oberon One. He'd introduced the good doctor to the element that had allowed their race to first manifest in this universe, and hinted at everything that could be accomplished with it. Even just the barest inkling of the element's potential was enough to inspire Toomey to stay in near-constant contact.

All of which meant that Kergan was in the catbird seat. The entity that shared their mind delighted in the term. Kergan had no idea what it meant, but it was fun to think about. *Catbird seat.* He would have to look it up on the network. He suspected it had something to do cats killing birds.

Dr. Toomey gave him an odd look, and the Kergan part of their mind said it likely meant he was uncomfortable with something. They definitely didn't want their new friend to be uncomfortable.

"Is everything all right, Doctor?"

Toomey frowned. "I hesitate to ask this, Officer, but I'm afraid I have to if I'm going to continue with my plan. I hope it doesn't sound ungrateful."

Kergan grinned again. "Ask away, my good man. That's how knowledge advances, isn't it?"

"Indeed." Toomey cleared his throat. "I appreciate the abstract Warden Farrell sent me on the... element that you've discovered. I've had the opportunity to scrutinize it, and it's quite literally the most fascinating discovery I've ever encountered—*if* it's true."

Kergan felt a little tug in his chest. What was this? Disappointment?

"I'm sorry, Doctor, I don't understand. What do you mean, *if* it's true?"

"Again, that's why I feared sounding indecorous. It's just that—well, I find myself having difficulty reconciling this information with someone of your background."

"Background?" The Kergan part of them bristled.

"A layman," Toomey said quickly. "Someone without an academic background, I mean."

"I know what you meant." Kergan's voice was cool now. "Still, I suppose I can't blame you. It's an extraordinary thing, after all. I would have thought the evidence of that modified Raft reaching Earth in such a short time would be enough to convince you—"

"It is, it is, of course." Toomey's eyes were more animated now than Kergan had ever seen them. He was showing emotion, which Kergan liked very much. "What I meant is, I'd very much like to see the element you're describing to me. For myself. Perhaps that would allow me to think of more supplies that might be of use to you in your endeavors."

Kergan felt his lips purse as he thought about the offer. He knew what he needed to build the wormhole generator. It would be simple once they had the Rafts working again, which would allow for more excavation of the element from the surface. He didn't need anything from this strange man, friend or not.

And yet... hadn't Sloane gained something from spending time with Dev Schuster? Obviously, it had ultimately led to his death at Kergan's hands, but Sloane seemed to gain inspiration from the human. Imagination, he called it. He'd said it was necessary for invention and innovation. Their species had always simply taken the technology they needed when they subjugated others. There was no need to create their own.

But Sloane had found it *fun* to do so. He would never have used that word, of course, but it was the truth. And above all else, Butch Kergan was *always* looking for fun.

"All right," he said, rising. "Excuse me for one moment."

He fetched a chunk of the element from a small pile on his desk and returned with it to the commlink. It glowed in his hand, emitting all the colors of the spectrum, and a few that didn't exist as such in the physical universe. He wondered how it appeared on the receiving end.

He didn't wonder long. Toomey's ratlike eyes bulged almost to normal human size.

"Extraordinary," he breathed.

"You believe me now, I take it?" Kergan asked with a smug grin.

"Of course, of course." Toomey's Adam's apple bobbed in his

narrow throat. "It's just that… if it's truly capable of everything in the abstract you sent me, this could be a turning point in human history."

Kergan could barely supress a giggle. "Oh, I think we can *definitely* say this is a turning point for humanity."

"The technology we could produce would be revolutionary," said the doctor.

Kergan had a sudden idea, one that sent a thrill of delight up his belly, the way mating with Iona Ridley had. He leaned forward in his seat, so that he was right up close to the holocamera.

"Not just revolutionary," he said. "World-changing. Perhaps even world-*ruling*, if you take my meaning."

Toomey's silent stare confirmed that he had, indeed, taken Kergan's meaning. This could lead to all sorts of fun.

I'm such a shit-disturber, he told himself. It was all he could do not to giggle with glee.

"This is why I asked you to kill Captain Quinn and the others. They have direct knowledge of this, and we wouldn't want them tattling about it to the general public, or worse, the government, now would we?"

"I still don't understand how you came across this knowledge," Toomey said after finally composing himself. Apparently, his curiosity wasn't going to allow him to just accept the gift.

Kergan sighed. He supposed that was the price one paid for imagination. It was time to let the cat out of the bag. And deep down, wasn't he actually looking for someone with whom he could share the truth? Who could share in his fun?

"Dr. Toomey," he said gravely. "There are a few things you need to know about me, and about Oberon One, if you're going to visit, and if we're going to continue our relationship."

Toomey nodded. "Of course."

"Excellent. First and foremost, Doctor, I must ask you a question: are you familiar with the concept of attenuation?"

21

Chelsea felt white-hot hatred in her chest for the man with Quinn's face, though she didn't understand exactly why. Sure, she should feel angry, but this was more severe. Was it *because* he'd appropriated the face? Why did that bother her so much?

Like that's my biggest worry right now, she chided herself. *Next stop for me is my father's office, but the next stop for everyone else is the morgue.*

She was standing beside Quinn, and caught him reaching behind himself for his pistol. But the man who called himself Zero simply smiled and shook his head.

"Don't be stupid. My associates here are armed with real weapons this time."

The other four were holding rifles that even Chelsea, with her limited knowledge of firearms, knew would definitely fire projectiles. Quite rapidly, from the looks of them.

Quinn tossed his machine pistol to the floor, glowering, and the others followed suit. Ulysses had left the shock rifle in the van. All of them raised their hands, and the women did the same.

"Who's your new friend?" Zero asked, raising his chin in Ben's direction.

"The pizza guy," said Quinn. "How did you find us? We could have been anywhere in the world, and yet you immediately sniffed us out in Rome."

"Rome?" Zero looked at Chelsea with theatrical confusion, and she felt her stomach turn. "But she told me you were headed for Sydney. I don't understand."

"Remember which one of us is untouchable," she warned. "I'm betting that suit of yours won't do much against a stomp kick to the balls."

He ignored the threat. "It was easy as pie, really. Your ankle bracelet led us to you."

Chelsea's heart dropped, and she suddenly felt faint. This was *her* fault. But she'd been so careful! They were in *Rome*, for God's sake! The stolen property capital of the world!

"But... how?"

"Global Families don't become as rich as they are by being stupid," Zero said with that shit-eating grin. "Or generous, for that matter—they don't like it when other people have their stuff. Most princesses like you know that when your parents give you anything, it's already been logged in your family's online property registry."

Chelsea wanted to kick herself. She'd never cared about her family's wealth growing up. Never gave a thought to money at all, really, because she was too busy living her life. Now she was paying the price for her ignorance.

"That fence in Rome knew the bracelet had to have come from one of the Big Ten," Zero continued. "So he looked it up to see what it was worth. The second he searched for something that was listed as belonging to you, it pinged your family servers and tagged his location. We offered the reward, and ten minutes later, we were in the air."

Quinn let out a hissing sigh. "That's how everyone found out you were with us, too. The fence talked."

Zero touched his nose. "You *are* a sharp one, Quinn. And word of a ten-million-credit bounty travels fast in a shithole like Rome. You could buy the whole city with that kind of scratch."

"Who *are* you?" Chelsea asked, exasperated. "Do you work for my father, or are you just mercenaries looking for a reward? Dad might be a lot of things, but he's not a cold-blooded murderer. I can't believe that he'd make murdering my friends part of the contract for catching me. So who's *really* behind you?"

She knew it was a show of bravado on her part. As much as she wanted to make it seem otherwise, Chelsea honestly didn't know whether her father was capable of murder or not. Nothing seemed certain anymore.

"I love this, keep it up," Gloom said out of nowhere. She was grinning, and her hands were clasped politely behind her back. Chelsea thought she looked like someone watching a particularly interesting political debate. As much as she liked Gloom, she was still a long way from understanding her.

Quinn ignored the comment. "I'd like the answer to that myself," he said. "Oscar Bloom didn't hire you to ambush us and kidnap Frank King two years ago, so who was it? I think you owe us that much before you kill us."

Zero's smile was condescending, and it made Chelsea want to punch him, even if he did have Quinn's face.

"Everything's black and white with you, isn't it?" he said. "I'm either a mercenary *or* a government agent. I was hired by a private citizen *or* a shadow ops agency. Why can't it be both, Quinn?"

"Either get to the fuckin' point or shut the hell up an' shoot us," Ulysses groaned. "This jawin' is gettin' on my nerves."

"Amen," said Maggott.

Now it was their turn to smile, and they all did, in sheer defiance of the fact they were about to be killed. Chelsea felt her heart almost burst with pride at this crazy gang of prisoners and misfits who had somehow become more important to her than her own family.

Zero scowled, obviously disappointed that they weren't showing fear.

"So stupid," he spat. "You think there's a government that runs the world? Sorry to be the one who pisses in your cereal, people, but there's only one thing that runs the world, and that's money. Whoever's got it makes the rules, and whoever doesn't has to follow them. That's what King couldn't get through his thick skull."

"And he was killed for it," said Quinn.

"Was he?" Zero cocked an eyebrow. "You saw the body, then?"

"Keep it going," Gloom said softly, prompting Chelsea to wonder if she was having some sort of dissociative episode. She didn't seem to grasp what was going on around her.

Quinn's gaze narrowed. "You're lying. Why would your masters want to keep King alive?"

Zero shrugged. "Why indeed? But that's beside the point right now. The question you *should* be asking is why *you* are all still alive."

"Apparently so you can talk us to death," said Schuster.

Gloom giggled beside him. "Good one, soldier boy."

"Marine," the Jarheads muttered in unison.

"Will you shut up?" Zero snapped. "You take all the fun out of this. Look, the only reason my men and I haven't killed you yet is because of what you said to me in Vegas, Quinn."

"What I said?" Quinn raised his eyebrows. "You mean about your raging case of cyborg pink eye clearing up?"

Zero took a deep breath and hissed it back out. Chelsea felt obscenely good watching him trying so hard to keep his cool.

"You told me there was a war coming," he said. "Said that you were going to need resourceful men to fight it. What did you mean by that?"

"It's the reason we broke out of Oberon One," said Quinn. "Didn't you ever ask yourself that question? Why we did it?"

Zero's expression was blank, but Chelsea got the sense that he was working hard to keep it that way.

"I bet it's killing you, isn't it?" Quinn taunted. "Why would the four men you set up in Astana align themselves with a Southern Saint and the daughter of a Global Family to break out of a prison two-and-a-half billion kilometers from Earth?"

"You have to admit, it goes against your character," said Zero. "You and your men accepted the verdict of treason with your typical stoicism. And yet two years later, you break out. It doesn't make sense."

"I guess you'll never know, seeing as how you're going to kill us."

"This is perfect," said Gloom.

"Shut up!" Zero snapped to Gloom. Then he turned back to Quinn. "This war you're talking about: who's behind it? How did you find out about it?"

"Factions?" Maggott scoffed. "What're ye, daft?"

"Stow it," said Quinn. "What do you think is behind it?"

Out of nowhere, one of Zero's men spoke through the speaker in his helmet.

"Tick tock, Zero," said an annoyed voice with an Australian accent. "Toomey said not to waste time on them."

Behind her, Chelsea heard Ben whisper to himself: "*Toomey?* What the hell...?"

Zero rolled his eyes and rounded on his men. "And *I* told you to keep your fucking mouths shut and follow orders." He turned back to Quinn. "Everyone knows the factions aren't really at peace. The Trilateral Government is just a gang of oligarchs taking over daily operations. So who's going to take the first shot this time?"

"Why do you care?" asked Quinn. "Trying to figure out who'll pay you the most?"

Zero grinned. "Guy's gotta eat."

"Really?" said Schuster. "I wasn't sure whether cyborgs had to eat."

"I'd appreciate if you told *your* minions to shut it, too," Zero sighed. "This is a conversation between us."

Chelsea heard Ulysses suck in air to protest, so she quickly touched his arm and shook her head. Now was *not* the time for arguing over who was in charge of whom.

"Here's what I'll tell you," said Quinn. "None of the factions are involved."

"Really? Who's going to be fighting the war, then?"

"Deez."

Zero frowned. "Deez? Who the hell is Deez?"

"Deez Nuts," Quinn said, flipping his middle finger to Zero, and Chelsea burst into helpless laughter along with the rest of her people. All except Gloom, who still seemed to be in her own world, and Ben, who still looked deep in thought.

"Okay, now you're just being a prick," said Zero.

He hoisted his rifle and aimed it squarely between Quinn's eyes, prompting Chelsea's heart to give a little kick. Her mind raced: should she try to get between the gun and Quinn? What would happen next? What could she do to keep her friends alive?

Then a sudden sound came from somewhere behind Gloom: a cartoonish "whoo-hoo!" that Chelsea found oddly familiar. She didn't have time to think about the bizarre interruption, though.

"Finally," said Gloom.

What...?

Gloom's hands emerged from behind her back, holding the device she'd been carrying around since Vegas. There was a green light flashing on a readout screen as she levelled it with both her hands in the direction of Zero and his men.

Then the green light flashed outward in a flat 360-degree wave, and the black suits fell to the floor. Chelsea watched as Zero's face connected squarely with the steel floor of FUBAR's cargo hold.

Gloom turned to Quinn. "That's *two* you owe me now."

22

Quinn blinked stupidly for a moment as he tried to process what had just happened.

"Don't stand there!" Gloom cried. "We need to get them off the ship *now*! We'll be lucky if we have thirty seconds!"

That got them all moving. Maggott knelt and hoisted one of the black suits over his shoulder. Quinn and Ulysses grabbed Zero by his arms and legs while Bishop, and Schuster took the one who had complained about wasting time. The three women dragged the fourth man out by his feet. They left all of them in a heap on the ground and double-timed back in to the ship.

The rear door lifted up as Schuster hit the pilot's seat and started up the engines. Quinn was right on his heels, followed by Gloom.

"All aboard!" Bishop shouted from the back, and Schuster hit the lifting thrusters at full power. The ship rose a hundred meters in less than ten seconds.

Quinn turned to Gloom, wide-eyed. "You told me in Vegas that gadget wouldn't work on them again!"

"Yeah, and I told you I upgraded it on the way to Rome!" She shook her head. "Try to keep up, will you? Why do you think I was so happy that you guys were yakking for as long as you were? The box was hunting for their frequency."

"So *that's* what that *woo-hoo* was!" Chelsea called from the cargo hold.

"When the box hit paydirt, it let me know and I broadcast the virus."

"Wait," said Schuster. "When did you write the virus? And how did you know which frequency to write a virus for?"

Gloom looked at him like he was dim. "I've got a thousand viruses ready at any given time. I took a particularly nasty one and made a few minor variations according to the various frequencies it might find its way in on."

Quinn shook his head. He had no idea what she was talking about, but that wasn't going to stop him from doing what he did next. He grabbed Gloom in a bear hug and squeezed.

"Totally not okay with this," she hissed nervously in his ear. "Just stop it, all right?"

He chuckled, but did as she asked. "You just got a field promotion, young lady. Consider yourself a Marine gunnery sergeant from now on."

She gave him a look he couldn't read, but there was no misinterpreting Schuster's glare.

"*A gunny?* It took me *two years* to make gunny! And I was in a fricking war!"

"The stakes are higher," said Quinn. "Now get your mind on your job. They'll be on our ass in no time."

As if on cue, a quartet of Rafts appeared on the long-range feed from below. It wouldn't take long for them to bridge the gap if FUBAR didn't get moving.

"Shit," said Quinn. "They each must have piloted their own ship and hidden them in the hills around us. What's out best option?"

"Suborbital parabolic incursion," said Schuster.

"Dev—"

"Get into space and open up the engines as much as we can

without causing environmental effects, then head back down to Earth. Everyone get in your seats and strap in."

"What if Zero and company do the same?" Gloom asked as she and the others buckled in.

"Once we're out of the atmosphere, they won't be able to keep up to FUBAR's engines."

"Let's do it," said Quinn. "Set a course for San Francisco. It's time we took the fight to them."

"Are you sure?" asked Chelsea.

"I don't know about the rest of you, but I'm sick of running. If we're going to go down, we're going to go down swinging. And if there's any chance we can get someone with some authority to listen to us, it's in the capital city."

"Hold on," said Schuster. "We're going to boost in twenty seconds."

The ship's attitude adjusted so that it was climbing on a steep incline, and Quinn could feel himself being pushed into his seat.

"Quinn!" Ben called from the back. "That guy back there, Zero! He said something that got me—"

The sentence was cut off by a shock wave that rattled the entire ship and sent Quinn's skull flying into the panel next to his seat. His vision doubled for a moment, but he was able to shake it off. On the monitor, he could see two Rafts gaining on them.

"Plasma blast," said Dev. "Straight up our tailpipe. They're pushing to catch up to us and force us down."

Another blast hit them, more glancing than the first but still enough to rock the ship. Quinn felt anger spreading through him. He had meant what he said about being sick of running. No one had ever retreated their way to victory in a war, and on a fundamental level, that's what he and the rest of them were: warriors.

"Dev," he said. "How'd you like to take the offensive for a change?"

Quinn couldn't see Schuster's face, but he could hear the smile in his voice. "I thought you'd never ask."

"Consider the order given."

"Yessir."

"Wait a minute—" Gloom began, but then FUBAR banked steeply to port and she seemed to forget what she was going to say.

The move caught their tail off-guard and the first two ships went screaming past where FUBAR had been. They were on the edge of the atmosphere now, with the Earth beneath them. Up here there were only satellites and the odd drop ship, but none of them were anywhere near right now. The sky was an open battlefield.

"Hold on tight," said Schuster, punching the thrusters again to take them higher, and suddenly they were above the four pursuing ships.

"Shouldn't we be mush against our seats by now?" asked Gloom. "I mean, there's still gravity pushing on us, right?"

"Inertia doesn't really obey the laws of physics on FUBAR," said Schuster. "I'll explain when we're not in a firefight."

He brought the ship around and back down, so that now they were behind the four ships. Quinn saw the little electronic bulls-eyes of the auto-targeting system floating around the monitor, showing them places that were just waiting to be shot.

"Put that thumb to work, Sergeant," said Quinn.

"Yessir."

Schuster flipped the locking mechanism off the top of the joystick, revealing the controls for FUBAR's plasma cannon. The targeting bulls-eyes swung through the screen for a moment before landing on the heat signature left by the engine of one of the Rafts. The nose on the monitor exploded in red fire as balls of superheated matter blasted forward, driving right through the main hull of the closest ship. It went up like a Roman candle, blowing outward and then receding as the lack of oxygen smothered the fire in a matter of seconds.

Watching the fireworks, Quinn felt a deep satisfaction that had been eluding him for years.

"Good shot, Dev!" Maggott crowed from the back. "Take that, ye wee bastards!"

"Yeah!" Ellie shouted. "What *he* said!"

Then the retaliation hit, and FUBAR shuddered so hard Quinn

thought it might fly apart. The monitors showed the remaining three Rafts had taken position on three points behind them, and judging by that last blast, they meant business.

"I think our playmates might have lost their concern for my well-being," said Chelsea. "They might have decided to just cut their losses."

"What does that mean?" asked Ellie.

"It means discretion is the better part of valor," said Bishop. "Unless you've got a hard-on to keep fighting, Lee?"

Quinn did, but he knew it wasn't the smart move. He checked their position on the monitors: they were well over the Atlantic.

"Dev, is there any way we can use the cloak again?"

"For a short time, yeah. It drained us dry the first time because we were coming off three weeks at interstellar speeds."

"Long enough to get us to San Francisco?"

"I think so."

Quinn nodded just as another blast shook the ship. "All right, let's set a course. When we engage, we'll hit the cloak. We can spend the rest of the trip getting those recordings out of the ship's computer and ready for Ben to broadcast."

"Yessir," said Schuster.

"Quinn!" Ben called. "I need to tell you about—"

Another blast, this time thunderous, and FUBAR didn't just shudder, it did a full 360. Alarm sounds went off in the bridge as Schuster struggled to pull it out of its tailspin.

"Shit!" Quinn barked. The readouts were dropping rapidly.

"That wasn't plasma," Schuster said with barely supressed alarm. "Shit! That was an electromagnetic pulse!"

Quinn snarled. Zero was nothing if not clever. If they couldn't catch them, he'd throw a monkey wrench at them.

"Damage?"

"The computer's struggling," said Schuster. "EMPs aren't as effective as they used to be back in the 2070s with the new shielding they developed, but we're going to lose auto-navigation at the very least."

"What was our heading when it hit?" Quinn asked.

"Eastern seaboard, why?"

Gloom nodded, excited. "I see what he's saying. If we stay on the course, we can still outrun them."

"Exactly," said Quinn. "Get ready to use the cloak and push the engines."

"Yessir." Schuster played with the controls, and suddenly the world went dark around them as light began to bend around the ship. The interior lights dimmed as the power drain suddenly shot up.

"Whoa," Gloom breathed. "We're seriously invisible?"

"Yup."

"Man, could I ever get into trouble with tech like this."

Schuster hit the engines and began a rapid descent, tripling their speed in the blink of an eye, and suddenly Quinn had a feeling of déjà vu, remembering back to their landing after the trip home from Oberon. His mind reeled at the thought that had been less than three days earlier.

"What was our exact heading?" Gloom asked.

"Asbury Park, New Jersey," said Schuster. "Why?"

"Okay, then, we'll survive."

"How do you know that?"

Gloom frowned. "Because God won't let me die on the Jersey Shore, if she knows what's good for her."

23

"They're in New Jersey," Zero said into the commlink. "I'm sure they think they've escaped."

"New Jersey?" Toomey's nose wrinkled in the holographic display. "It was fortunate you had the foresight to put a tracking device in their ship, Zero, considering they managed to subdue you with the exact same method they used in Las Vegas."

"I knew they'd do something like that," Zero lied. "It was all part of the plan to get them somewhere where we could more easily collect the ship, just like you ordered."

"Mm. Of course. Where are you now?"

Zero fought against the anger rising in his chest. He didn't like being made a fool of, and having to jump through Toomey's hoops in the aftermath of it was galling. But he had to bide his time.

"I'm at the Manhattan shipyards, getting what you asked for," he said. "It'll be ready to go in about thirty minutes."

"Will you need another man to replace the one you lost?"

"Albright wasn't a *loss*," said Zero. "He deserved to get shot down. He was an idiot and a liability."

"Just because you didn't like him didn't mean he was a liability."

The anger flared more brightly. "He said your name in front of Quinn and his people, Doctor. Does *that* make him a liability?"

The look of shock on Toomey's gaunt face was supremely satisfying.

"How did you let that happen?" he snapped. It was the first time the doctor had ever raised his voice in Zero's presence.

"And how exactly could I have stopped him?" Zero growled. "Do you have some method of controlling another person's mind that you haven't told me about?"

Toomey blanched. "Of course not," he sputtered. "Don't be ridiculous."

"*You're* the one wondering why I can't control others," said Zero, wondering what was going through the man's head. "Look, let's move on. Let Quinn think he's gotten a reprieve. It'll make it that much easier to take them down when we're ready."

"Wait," said Toomey. "We need to rethink this."

That was it. Zero felt his frustration finally reach the boiling point.

"Rethink what?" he barked. "First it was retrieve the Bloom woman, kill the others. Then it was retrieve the woman *and* the ship, and kill the others. Now you're changing the plan again!"

"I have to know what Quinn knows!" said Toomey, with an edge that Zero had never heard before. Was he actually nervous? Zero hadn't believed the man capable of emotions.

"Knows about *what?*"

Toomey paused. "The ship, of course. And whether he recognized my name. If he knew that I was involved with you, and if he told that to anyone else—"

"How the hell would he know about you?" Zero shook his head. "You're the ghost that other ghosts tell stories about around the campfire, for Christ's sake!"

"We can't take that chance." Toomey had regained his composure. "Bring me the Bloom woman, the ship *and* Quinn."

Zero grit his teeth. "You want fucking takeout while I'm at it?" he hissed.

"Don't be ridiculous. The trip is too long for that. Notify me when you've arrived in San Francisco."

The holographic sphere containing Toomey's head winked off, leaving Zero to punch the bridge wall of his Raft, leaving a dent in the steel the size of a small plum.

24

"Ach," Maggott groaned. "Me arse smelled better'n this place after three weeks in fookin' space."

Chelsea could have done without the imagery, but there was no arguing with the sentiment. The shoreline was fetid, black with raw sewage and other waste flowing into it from the teeming slums of New York via the Hudson River. FUBAR sat precariously in the sand and garbage, protected—if it could be called that—by the camouflage hologram projection. Luckily for them, Schuster had been able to bring her down in an area that even the locals wouldn't spend any time near. The downside, of course, was that they themselves had to be there.

Schuster and Gloom were examining the rear starboard area of the ship, where the EMP had struck, for damage. The rest of them were in the cargo hold with Chelsea, waiting for word on damage before deciding what they would do next.

"Cain't we close the damn door?" Ulysses moaned.

"It's not fair for Dev and Gloom to have to smell this and not us," said Quinn. "They're doing all the work."

Ulysses shook his head. "Think I'll go to the shitter fer a breath o' fresh air."

"Hey, I grew up around here," said Quinn.

"What's yer point?"

Quinn frowned. "Guess I don't actually have one."

Chelsea looked up as Schuster and Gloom came around the rear of the ship. The looks on their faces didn't fill her with hope.

"How bad is it?" asked Quinn.

"Navigation is salvageable," said Schuster. "It looks like the brunt of the damage wasn't to the operating systems."

Chelsea raised an eyebrow. "That's good, isn't it?"

"The damage is in data storage," said Gloom. "That's where the ship's records are."

Her stomach dropped. "So you're saying..."

"We don't know if we'll be able to retrieve the recordings we need for broadcast."

Bishop and Ellie turned to Ben, who was sitting between them.

"What do you think?" asked Bishop. "Is there any other way to do this if we can't recover those records?"

Ben heaved a sigh and held up his hands in surrender. "I've been trying to wrap my head around a lot for the last ninety minutes or so," he said. "The short answer is probably yes, we do need to have that data. But I've been thinking about something else since we were first ambushed by those men in black in Rome."

Quinn shook his head. "Sorry, Ben, you were trying to get my attention but I was a bit distracted. What did you want to talk about?"

"That guy with your face—"

"It's a long story," Quinn sighed. "Call him Zero."

"Zero, okay. Anyway, one of his men said something about someone named Toomey."

Chelsea nodded. "I remember that. Do you know what it meant?"

"I don't know, but I think I might have a clue. Dr. Toomey was a name I heard over and over again when I was investigating the Prometheus black site in Antarctica. He was the head of the entire operation, according to my sources."

"Are ye fookin' kiddin me?" asked Maggott. "Does that mean Prometheus was behind what happened t'us in Astana?"

"One step at a time, big guy," said Quinn, clearly confused. "What's his connection with you, Chelsea?"

"I've never heard the name before," she said, racking her brain for any memory of her father ever talking about Prometheus.

"Whatever the connection is, it just proves the conspiracy," said Ben. "I mean, after being through what I've been through with you folks, I believe what you say. This just confirms it."

"Except it raises more questions instead of answering them," said Ellie. "Was this Dr. Toomey behind those men killing Major Zheng? If so, why? And what's it got to do with us and Chelsea?"

Quinn ran his hands down his face and rubbed his eyes. "I really just want a break," he sighed. "Every time we turn around, there's another problem to be solved."

Chelsea felt her heart cramp as the reality of their situation hit home. They'd been on Earth for three days, overcome ridiculous challenges, and they didn't seem any closer to accomplishing their goal than they were when they'd started. If anything, they were just more confused.

"What's that sound?" asked Gloom.

"What sound?" But as soon as the words were out of Chelsea's mouth, she heard it too. "Is it thunder?"

They all stood and looked around them. The volume was increasing by the second. Finally, Ulysses pointed north, over New York Harbor.

"What the hell izzat?" he said, raising his voice to be heard over the noise.

A few moments later, the source of the noise had grown considerably. It was a ship, bigger than anything Chelsea had seen outside of orbit, and it was headed right toward them.

"Jesus!" Bishop cried. "Look at the size of it!"

A moment later, three smaller ships emerged from behind the behemoth and sped low along the water, crossing the miles between them at a speed that sent arcs of water flying up around them.

"Scatter!" Quinn ordered. "Get out of here, now!"

"What about the ship?" asked Schuster.

"Leave it, just get out of here!"

The others did as they were ordered, but Chelsea stood her ground. Quinn grabbed her shoulder and tried to pull her along with him, but she broke free from his grasp.

"Come on!" he yelled. "Let's go!"

"No!" She took a deep breath. "This is all about me. They're just going to keep coming until they get me. At least this way, you all have a chance of getting away!"

Quinn locked eyes on hers and took her hands in his.

"I'm not going to let them take you!"

"You don't have a choice!"

She fought back tears, knowing what he was going through. She didn't want to be separated from him and the others, either, but it was the only way. She knew that Zero and his men would never stop, and even if they did, there would always be someone else out there ready to collect the bounty on her head.

The two turned toward the beach and saw the others cresting a hill, sprinting into the garbage heaps that surrounded the shoreline. They could hide in there for days if need be.

"Go!" she yelled. "Get out of here before it's too late!"

Quinn stood his ground. "Where you go, I go."

"They might kill you!"

The roar became deafening as the massive ship closed in on them, kicking up waves and clouds of sand as it descended over the shoreline and onto the beach. She reached out and clutched Quinn's hand tight. It was the only thing she could think of to do.

The three smaller ships drew up alongside the behemoth, finally coming to rest beside it on the sand. A gangplank lowered from the side hatch of the lead ship, and when the door opened, Chelsea wasn't surprised to see a man in a black body suit with Quinn's face emerge. He strode toward them with a smug grin on his false face, as if he had all the time in the world.

"Playtime finally over?" he asked when he was within earshot. "And look at you, Quinn, being a knight in shining armor."

"Kiss my ass," said Chelsea.

"Why the giant ship?" asked Quinn. "You need something that big just to take on a handful of fugitives?"

Zero grinned. "I don't even see a handful, I just see two." He waved a hand at two others in black, who Chelsea assumed were the ones from Rome. "Find the others and kill them."

"No!" she cried. "You've got me! You don't need them!"

"You're right, I don't," he said. "But they pissed me off."

Quinn squeezed her hand and looked her in the eye. Something about that look helped calm her. If he was keeping his head, she could keep hers.

He turned back to Zero. "Are you going to kill me, too?"

Zero snorted a laugh. "Of course not. You and I have a lot more business together. Speaking of that, shall we?" He raised a hand in the direction of the ship he'd landed in.

Chelsea didn't understand. "Why did you bring that huge ship?"

"That?" Zero looked at it absently. "That's going to bring your ship along to San Francisco. That way we can be assured that you're not going to take off in it again."

She and Quinn exchanged a startled glance. "Why the hell do you want the ship?" he asked.

"Because from what I've seen, she's pretty darn special," said Zero. "And there are some people who'd really like to take a closer look at her when we arrive in San Francisco."

Chelsea felt cold dread creeping into her guts and she clutched Quinn's hand and began the walk down the beach, toward Zero's ship and whatever fate had in store for them next.

~

Ulysses breathed through his mouth as he peered out from his vantage point in the garbage heaps that had long ago become inextricably merged with the sand dunes and sea oats. He watched as the drop ship took off with Quinn and Chelsea aboard, and as a handful of men in uniforms began attaching cables to FUBAR. The cables in turn were attached to a series of small vehicles with tank treads to allow them to navigate along the sand and pull the ship into the cargo hold of the much bigger one.

Meanwhile, there were three men in black suits and ugly rifles searching the dunes for them.

"Open t'idears," he whispered to Geordie Bishop, who was hunkered beside him under the trash. The rest of them were huddled a couple of meters lower down on the same hill.

"I think it's safe to assume the others are headed for San Francisco," said Bishop. "The fact that Zero didn't kill Quinn outright is a good sign, or at least a sign that Quinn has something he wants."

"I meant fer us. Them boys in black is lookin' to kill us."

"Look, Ulysses, you and Gloom and Ben have done your part. You can take them and make a run for it, get the hell out of here. None of you owe us anything."

"What about you?"

"We follow Quinn, always. We can try to draw their fire while the rest of you escape. Whatever we choose, the three of us have to try to get on that ship before it takes off. Barring that, we find some other transportation to San Francisco. That's assuming we can evade those men in black, of course."

The sound of gunfire rang through the dunes, and Bishop held up a hand to keep the others quiet. They couldn't risk giving away their position, especially since these guys seemed to be trigger-happy and shooting at anything that moved.

Ulysses frowned and ran a hand over his chin. "What if there wuz another way?" He turned so that the others could see and hear him better. "This ain't sump'n I'd suggest in any other situation, but I don't think we got a choice here. But we gotta be all in on this; everyone's gotta agree."

A few minutes later, the two men had worked out a plan. It was desperate, and incredibly dangerous, and they wished there was another way, but in the end, it was their only viable option. They each sent up a little prayer to whatever god might be listening before they went to talk to the others.

~

"How long are we supposed to wait for them?" asked the petty officer, glancing at his wrist display.

They were done loading the Raft on board the heavy transport ship, affectionately known among the New Jersey Coast Guard as the Kraken, though he still had no idea why they were doing it. Their orders were to get the Raft on board and hand over the controls to the men in black suits, who would take things from there. The Kraken's flight plan had already been programmed in.

The sound of sporadic gunfire had been echoing through the trash hills a few hundred meters away for the last twenty minutes, which made them both nervous. The two had their sidearms, but they had also seen the wicked rifles the men in black had been carrying when they headed into the dunes, and wanted nothing to do with them.

"Takeoff is supposed to be at noon," said the chief warrant officer, an older lady who had joined him and the three seamen assigned to the task. "I don't know what we're supposed to do if they're not back by then. It's not like we can just leave the ship sitting here."

She was just about to commlink in to New Jersey Command when she saw the black figures march onto the sand from behind a series of dunes. There were three of them walking behind four other people in civilian clothes.

"Orders didn't say anything about taking on passengers," said the petty officer.

"Best not question it," said the chief. "These guys get their orders from someone way above either of our pay grades, sailor."

Once the group was close enough to make out details, they saw the four civilians were wearing "shockles," which was the colloquial term for wrist restraints tethered to an electrified belt. There were two women and two men. One of the women, a redhead, looked frightened, while the other, a younger brunette, was fuming mad. One man wore dreadlocks and a curious expression, but the one that stood out most was a giant, with close-cropped hair and the beginnings of a beard, sporting a scowl that could put the run on a mountain lion.

These weren't passengers, they were prisoners.

The chief saluted the men in the black smart suits when they arrived, figuring it was better to be safe than sorry. Their mirrored helmet visors gave her the creeps.

"Ship's good to go whenever you're ready to take over," she said. "Uh, sir."

The men in black jammed the muzzles of their weapons into the backs of the civilians to prod them in the direction of the Kraken's gangplank.

"There's three dead back there in the shit piles," said one of them through the radio in their helmet.

The Coast Guard officers shared a glance. "Uh, our orders were to supervise the loading and then get back to base," said the chief.

"Find the bodies and burn them," said the lead man in black.

"Don't ye fookin' touch 'em!" the giant howled. He suddenly strained against his shockles, and for a moment the officers were sure he was going to break free. But one of his captors activated the electric charge in the belt and the big man dropped to his knees in the sand, grunting. The redhead screamed, but was quickly silenced by a rifle muzzle between her shoulder blades.

With that, two of the men in black grabbed the giant by his arms and hauled him, staggering, to his feet. They finished their march up the gangplank in silence.

"Holy shit," the petty officer whispered once the hatch had sealed shut behind the strange group. "Whaddaya figure this is all about, Chief?"

"I don't figure anything," said the chief. The Kraken's mighty engines roared to life, causing the sand and trash to swirl around them as it began to thrust upward into the sky. "All I know is I don't want those fucking spooks tracking me down, so we're going to find those bodies and burn them, just like the man said. Then I'm going to go back to base, keep my head down, do my job, and count the days until I can retire."

The petty officer took a deep breath and let it out again. "Aye, ma'am. Let's get this over with."

They had no idea then that neither of them would ever come close to drawing their military pension. But they would realize it soon enough.

25

Zero's jump ship was faster than the Raft he'd been flying since Quinn's return to Earth, and it was on a priority flight path, which meant it would take them about forty-five minutes to reach San Francisco. Then he could finally put paid to this fucking assignment.

Still, it had been fun playing cat-and-mouse with Quinn, and there was time left for a little more, too. He let the autopilot take control and turned his seat around the face Quinn and Chelsea Bloom, who were strapped into the seats in the rear of the ship's small bridge, their wrists and ankles restrained. Zero was taking no risks this time.

"Ever been to San Francisco?" he asked. Quinn simply glared at him. "Not that you'd recognize it, even if you had. You've been in prison since before they started the transformation. Ever since it was designated as the Trilateral capital, it's changed completely. The air is clean, the trash and sewage have been cleared away. I know that we call some of the nicer places in the world Utopia Cities, but really, even they still have slums. But not the City by the Bay. It's the real deal."

"And me without my holocamera," Quinn said drily.

"What have you told my father?" asked Chelsea. "I'm curious. How much does he know about us? About what you've been doing to my friends and me?"

"He knows all he needs to," Zero said. "That you've been apprehended and will be with him shortly."

"What about the others?"

Zero shrugged. "What about them? Your father hasn't asked about any of them, and I don't offer information. Comes with the job."

"I'm betting you'll immediately separate us when we get to San Francisco," said Quinn. "Chelsea goes to her family, and I go where?"

"Oh, I'm sure we can find someplace where you'll be of use."

"We?" Quinn cocked an eyebrow. "You mean you and Toomey."

Zero's heart jumped a bit, but he didn't let it show. He'd expected it to come up eventually, as a desperate play by Quinn to sound like he knew more than he really did. Zero frowned and put on a blank look, which was easy now that he was wearing his regular, bland face.

"I'm afraid you lost me," he said. "What's a Toomey?" He paused when he heard how that sounded out loud and quickly added: "Is this a joke? Now you say, 'Nothing, what's it to *you?*'"

"Sorry, I should have been clearer," Quinn said amiably. "I'm talking about Dr. Toomey. You know, used to be the head of the Prometheus black site in Antarctica before it got shut down? He's been in the wind for a while, working undercover for the highest bidder."

Zero stared at him, his mind scrambling for something to say, a way to respond. How the *hell* did Quinn know who Toomey was? There was no way he could have extrapolated that just from what Albright had let slip on the ship in Rome, and he couldn't have stumbled across it online; anything that referenced Toomey on the network was deeply encrypted.

"What makes you think I know who you're talking about?" he said at last.

Quinn leaned back in his seat and closed his eyes. "If you're just going to waste my time, I might as well nap for the rest of the trip."

Zero looked at Chelsea Bloom, who simply shrugged. "I'll make sure to bring it up with my father."

He turned his chair back to face the monitors in order to hide the frustration raging through him. This whole thing was supposed to be as easy as the ambush in Astana, and yet here they were, days later, with Quinn still holding cards even as a prisoner. Zero was finally forced to accept the fact that the man was a serious opponent, and that underestimating him could lead not only led to humiliation but, ultimately, defeat.

But what was the next move in this chess game? How could Zero get himself back to being a step ahead, not just of Quinn but of Toomey as well?

He took a deep breath and turned the pilot's seat back to face his captives, though he was starting to believe it was stupid of him to think of them that way.

"Fine," he sighed. "You're right, Quinn. I'm working with Toomey."

"Of course you are. He gave you that flexible face and your cyborg implants."

Zero clamped his jaw tight to hold in the anger that blazed through him like wildfire. He had made his living with his wits long before his physical enhancements, and he would not allow himself to be knocked off balance by anyone, let alone Quinn.

"What's your point?" he asked, keeping his voice even.

Quinn leaned forward in his seat as far as he could with the restraints and locked his gaze on Zero's.

"My point is that you need to listen to me. Will you?"

Zero snorted a laugh. "I was trying to listen to you in Rome and you blew me off with a sophomoric joke."

"If you'll recall, I followed it up with throwing a glitch into you and your buddies' super suits."

"If you're going to—"

"Will you shut up?" Quinn snapped. "This isn't some sort of high school rivalry, you idiot! We could have killed you and your men in Rome, all we had to do was grab your weapons when your suits went

on the fritz and blow your heads off, *but we didn't.* Just like I didn't kill you at the hangar in Vegas."

"All right!" Zero leapt out of his seat. "I get it, Quinn! We've been playing cat-and-mouse for the better part of three days and neither of us is winning! And you keep telling me you've got something to say, so just fucking say it already and put me out of my misery!"

Quinn glanced at the Bloom woman, who nodded.

"All right," he said. "Here goes. Have you or Toomey asked yourselves why we broke out of Oberon One?"

"I don't really care about why," Zero said blandly. "People in my line of work rarely do."

That seemed to throw Quinn a bit, which was more satisfying to Zero than it probably should have been.

"All right," said Quinn. "I'll come at this from a different angle. How did we get here from Uranus in three weeks?"

"Three weeks?" Zero peered at Quinn, as if he could somehow see right into the man's mind. "That's impossible."

"And yet here we are," said Chelsea Bloom.

"Our ship used a cloaking device while we were hemmed in by your formation in orbit," said Quinn. "We were invisible, not just from sensors but from their very eyes."

Zero frowned as he remembered Albright's complaint that Quinn's ship had disappeared. He'd dismissed it as incompetence—was it possible Albright had been telling him the truth?

"All right," he said. "Let's say I believe you, and somehow you were able to get here twice as fast as any ship I know of—"

"More than twice as fast," said Bloom.

Zero threw his head back. "Yes, fine, whatever! *How did you do it?*"

"There were modifications made to the ship by the engineering staff at Oberon One," said Quinn. "Speed and invisibility are just the one we know about; there are probably more."

"Modifications? On a space prison billions of kilometers from Earth? By prison engineering techs?"

"I know it sounds crazy—"

"Oh, no, not at all," Zero said sarcastically. "Makes perfect sense to me."

Quinn sighed. "I'll start from the beginning: my men and I were on the surface of Oberon about six weeks ago sounding for palladium deposits when a pair of meteorites hit the surface. In the commotion, something happened to the two guards who were with us, Sloane and Kergan."

"'Something happened.'" Zero threw up his hands. "Well, that explains it."

"Something took over their minds," Quinn said emphatically. "An alien intelligence that has access to highly advanced technical knowledge."

Zero was silent.

"The intelligence took over more minds and turned people into drones. They upgraded the Rafts to the extent that they could with existing technology. Then we went back down to the surface and dug out this element that no one had ever heard of before."

Still Zero said nothing.

"Sloane said that the element could be used to create all sorts of technology that we can't even dream of, and he built a device that took over every mind on the station. The six of us were the only ones who escaped. Now Kergan and his drones are building a machine that will open a wormhole to another star system and bring an army of aliens with highly advanced technology into our system. They're going to attack Earth and take over the minds of the human race, and the only way we can stop them is by uniting the entire planet in a concerted effort against them. *That's* the war I was warning you about."

Quinn finally stopped talking, and Zero gazed deep into the man's eyes for almost a full thirty seconds, unblinking.

"Well?" Quinn asked.

Zero sighed. "You know, I really did hold out some hope that we could have a rational discussion."

Bloom opened her mouth to protest, but Zero activated the electroshock generators built into both passenger seats. His guests suddenly went stiff, and Bloom's hair stood up for a few moments as their bodies dealt with the massive, sudden voltage running through them. Finally, their heads lolled to the side as they passed out.

"The least you could have done was come up with a plausible story," Zero muttered as he turned back to the controls. According to the readouts, they were about fifteen minutes from San Francisco Bay.

26

Quinn and Bloom were still unconscious when the ship descended over San Francisco, and Zero's mood was still as black as the body suit he wore.

The city was, as always, dazzling in the afternoon sunshine, but he didn't have the time or the inclination to enjoy it. He aimed the ship straight for the bay, bringing it in low under the restored Golden Gate Bridge and kicking up sluices of Pacific ocean on either side as he guided her toward a particular outcropping of rock. Once he reached it, he activated a control on the ship's panel and suddenly the rock winked out of existence, replaced by an opening about forty meters wide by twenty meters tall.

He guided the ship into the hangar bay of Toomey's private headquarters, where a computer automatically latched onto the controls via remote and landed the ship while Zero unbuckled his two guests. His enhanced cyborg musculature, aided by the servos in his smart suit, allowed him to hoist both of them over his shoulders and carry them effortlessly into the bay and the hallway beyond.

No one met him, which was as it should be. Almost all of Toomey's little sanctuary was automated, allowing him to have as few humans as possible present. Secrecy was as much a part of what he and Toomey did as electricity, and the number of human staff was kept to a bare minimum.

As he reached the room that would serve as Quinn and Bloom's cell, Zero picked up an audio call from Toomey on his wrist.

"When will the ship arrive?" the older man said without preamble.

"Hello to you, too, Doctor," said Zero. He laid the two bodies on a pair of sofas that faced each other in the expansive room. "I have Chelsea Bloom and Napoleon Quinn, as ordered. They're unconscious and in the private guest quarters." That was code for detention cell.

"Yes, excellent, but what about the ship?" The urgency in Toomey's voice was mildly alarming.

"The Coast Guard transport can barely make Mach 1, laden as it is," said Zero. "They don't call it the Kraken for nothing. It's scheduled to arrive at 1520 hours, a little over two and a half hours from now, at Angel Island."

There was silence for several moments, long enough for Zero to wonder if the connection had been terminated.

"You will meet the Raft when it lands and bring it here," he said finally. "None of the other staff are to be allowed on board."

"What about the ones who were captured in New Jersey?" Zero had received a text message from his men that they had killed two of Quinn's men and the professional criminal, and captured the giant and the other three during a firefight on the beach after he had taken off with Bloom and Quinn. "I assume you want them brought in as well?"

"It doesn't matter; they're obviously familiar with the ship. For that reason, you will need to dispose of them once we've extracted any information."

Zero sneered and raised his middle finger at his wristband. *Dispose of this, you prick.*

"I'll keep you apprised," he said, eager to end the conversation. "Zero out."

He gave the unconscious Quinn and Bloom a final glance before exiting the room and activating the lock. He would leave it to Toomey to get in touch with whatever intermediary he was using to communicate with Oscar Bloom and tell him that his daughter had finally arrived. He thought about the reward he was about to receive, and what he might do with it, but try as he might, his mind kept wandering back to Quinn and his ridiculous story about aliens taking over the Oberon One prison station.

At best, it was a ridiculous fabrication. At worst, it was the fevered imagination of a madman. Twenty years in the intelligence and clandestine operations fields had shown Zero that there was no shortage of insane people in the world. Not to mention the fact that Quinn and his men had been wrongfully convicted of treason, the worst crime imaginable to a Marine, and had spent two years locked up in deep space.

Zero ambled down the wide, low hallway, passing by several different laboratories that were in the midst of any number of automated experiments. As Toomey was so fond of saying, innovation doesn't follow the clock.

Treason. He couldn't seem to get the word out of his head. He had been personally responsible for setting up Quinn, for essentially ruining his life and those of his men, and Quinn *knew* it. And yet he hadn't taken revenge. He could have easily killed Zero at the hangar in Vegas and in Rome, and yet he hadn't.

Why hadn't he?

The question would consume his thoughts for the next two hours as he first travelled to the Angel Island airstrip and then waited for the behemoth ship known as the Kraken to land.

~

THE THREE ESCORT ships landed first in a semi-circle while Toomey's computers locked onto the Kraken and brought it to rest on the empty tarmac. Zero reflected absently on how, just two years earlier, the island had been hip-deep in waste that had floated in from the bay over the course of two generations. And yet here it was today, with a 500-square-meter landing pad that wasn't just free from debris, it was utterly pristine and once again teeming with life. As much as he despised the man, Zero had to respect Toomey's genius and the work he'd done with Prometheus.

The big ship came to rest in the center of the landing pad and Zero remotely opened the cargo hold doors. A pair of towing drones that had been standing by automatically rolled forward into the hold and positioned magnetic lifters under the Raft to begin the process of removing it.

He watched as the hatch opened on the first of the three escort ships to land, and one of his men prodded the four prisoners down the gangplank. They looked tired and hungry, which he supposed was to be expected.

Suddenly a light flashed on his wrist display, indicating an incoming text message. It was from Hines, the man who had taken over as his second when Albright was killed in space on their way from Rome back to the States. It was also the man who was bringing him his prisoners.

Zero looked at the message: *Suits fried, all three locked in. Who can extract.* He rolled his eyes and glared at Hines' mirrored visor. "I told you all to change suits before we left for Rome, but you wouldn't fucking listen."

Hines shrugged, prompting a chuckle from the giant, Maggott, despite his beaten-down demeanor.

"Fookin' texting," he sighed. "Need me t'tuck ye in, wee bairns?"

"Hey, *I* text," griped the younger woman, the one who'd zapped them both times with her tech. Hines responded with a cuff across the back of her head.

Zero resisted the urge to smack all of them. "Get to the maintenance bots once you lock these ones in the guest room," he snapped. "Have the suits tagged for maintenance, then report for debriefing."

Hines and the other two nodded, then drove the prisoners toward the lowered cargo hold doors on the Raft, which had already been extracted by the drones. Zero thought about what a production it had been to get the goddamned thing on, compared to how easy it had been to take it off. Technology really did make a huge difference in the quality of life. If only it didn't have to come from creeps like Toomey.

That sent his mind back to Quinn's story about Oberon One, and that brought with it the beginnings of a real bitch of a headache.

THEY FLEW in silence from Angel Island to Toomey's hideaway, Zero's men by necessity and the others due to exhaustion. After they had landed the Raft in the hangar, the men drove the four prisoners off the ship and into the headquarters. All four were stumbling noticeably by the time they reached the room where Zero had left Quinn and Bloom earlier.

The door slid open in response to his flashed command, and Hines and the others shoved the black man and the women into the room. In Maggott's case, they poked him in the back with their rifles, not wanting to throw out their backs, and he shuffled in obediently, for a change.

His first two prisoners had come to at some point and were glaring at Zero and his men.

"You're all together again," Zero said with mock delight. "Well, except for a few of you who apparently couldn't make it. I guess you'll have to play three-on-three from now on."

"Maggott," Quinn began, but the big man shook his head before he could continue.

"Sorry, sir," he said in a weak voice. "They dinnae make it. They drew the bastards' fire, but we got caught anyway." Tears trickled out of the corners of his eyes. "M'too fookin' big to hide..."

Ellie took his arm and stroked it. "It's okay," she soothed. "Shhh. It's all right. We're here now."

Quinn rounded on Zero with sudden energy, his eyes blazing.

"Some day, you're going to pay for this," he growled. "I don't know how or when or where, but it *will* happen."

Zero grinned. "You mean when you've got some down time from battling the alien army that's trying to take over our brains?"

While Quinn fumed, Zero's men in black exchanged blank, mirrored looks with each other. Hines tapped out a message on his wrist and the light on Zero's own wrist flashed, but he didn't bother to read it. He was in no mood to explain himself.

"Forget about it," he grumbled. "It's just a joke. Get those fucking suits off and then assemble for debriefing. I'll contact you when I'm ready."

He stalked out of the room and called Toomey on audio. He picked up immediately.

"Status?"

"The Raft is in the hangar," said Zero. "No one but my men and I have had access to it. It's all yours."

"Excellent. I'll be there presently. Toomey out."

"Wait."

"What is it?" Toomey's voice was terse.

"I want to be there when you take a look at that thing," he said. "I want to see all these upgrades for myself."

Toomey didn't respond for several seconds. "Why?" he asked finally. "You won't be able to understand any of it."

"Because I'm the one who did all the fucking work to get it, *and* your prisoners, here in one piece." He thought about that for a moment. "Well, most of them, anyway. The important ones. So I deserve to see what I worked so hard for."

"Fine," Toomey sighed petulantly. "I'll meet you there. Do *not* touch anything before I arrive."

The connection ended without another word, and Zero had already made up his mind to touch every single thing he could find in the Raft before Toomey got there.

27

Chelsea's chest hitched as the sobs threatened to close her throat. Her heart felt like a rock in her chest, and it was all she could do to keep from dropping to her knees on the floor. She'd managed to hold it in while Zero was in the room—it was bad enough his men were still here, but she refused to give *him* the satisfaction of seeing her cry—but now that he was gone, the grief rose in her like a wave that threatened to drown her. To her right, Quinn was snarling hard, his face crimson as his eyes welled with tears of his own.

"It's all my fault," she husked. "I'm so sorry. If I hadn't—"

Gloom grabbed her by the shoulders and gave her a shake. "Rein it in there, princess." She turned to the men in black. "Will you hurry up? They're in bad shape here."

Chelsea's raw eyes widened as Maggott rose from the floor and wiped his face, seemingly fully recovered from his breakdown. Meanwhile, the lead man in black crossed his arms over his chest and propped the ass of his smart suit against the arm of the sofa where she had recovered from her electroshock.

"Aw, c'mon now," said a familiar voice through the helmet radio. "I wanna see if'n Quinn's gonna shed any tears fer *me*."

The middle man, the tallest of the three, tugged on his helmet and a moment later, Chelsea was looking at Geordie Bishop. She forgot to breathe as Dev Schuster's face appeared under another helmet. Finally, the third man relented and doffed his own headgear, revealing a dark, chiseled face that Chelsea had seen on the other side of a polycarbonate cell door less than a month earlier.

"Buh," she said. "Whuh...?"

Beside her, Quinn's face had dropped with astonishment.

"How the hell...?" he breathed.

"The hunted became the hunters," said Bishop, slapping him on the shoulder. "We knew there was no way to make it off that beach without being seen, so Ulysses suggested we don't even try. We picked off Zero's men one by one, stole the suits and made it look like these four surrendered."

Ulysses bowed theatrically from the waist. "No applause, jes throw money."

Gloom frowned and crossed her arms over her chest. "For the record, Ellie, Ben and I thought they were nuts."

"I think all of you are nuts," said Ben, holding his hands wide in surrender. "But I'll tell you what, it's never boring with you people."

Chelsea and Quinn shared a look of supreme relief, then turned back to their friends. She could feel helpless giggles threatening to take the place of the sobs that had incapacitated her only moments before.

Quinn wrapped an arm around Bishop's neck and pulled him into a hug.

"You ever do something like this again, I'll fucking kill you myself," he growled into his friend's ear.

"So, just to be clear, you don't want to be rescued anymore?" Bishop replied.

"You know what I mean." He shook his head, laughing softly. "All right, now that Chelsea and I have officially aged ten years in the last two minutes, what's our status?"

"Zero had FUBAR brought into the hangar in this fortress, or whatever the hell this place is," said Schuster. His thick, blue-black hair was standing up from its time locked inside the helmet. "This Toomey guy is going to take a look at it."

"Makes sense," said Ben. "If Toomey really is the former head of Prometheus, then he'll be salivating over those tech upgrades. We need to get down there as soon as possible if we're going to recover those records and put them on the network before he gets to them."

"If the records are still intact," Quinn pointed out. "Dev and Gloom said they weren't sure if they were damaged before Zero and that huge ship arrived to steal FUBAR."

"What do we do if they're not there?" asked Ellie. "What's our Plan B?"

Bishop wrapped an arm around her shoulder and grinned. "We're the Jarheads of Oberon, baby. We don't do Plan B, we just find the craziest option and put all our chips on that."

"If I can get to a terminal and hack into the network, I should be able to set up a back channel to the Foster Kenya feed," said Gloom. "As long as we've actually got something to broadcast, that is."

"Long as us three got these here suits, we can get around the hallways," said Ulysses. "Why not head for the ship right now?"

Quinn looked around at each of them in turn and nodded. "All right," he said. "We're going for broke here. Anybody not in, say so right now and you can stay here."

They all gave him a quizzical look, except for Gloom, who rolled her eyes. Chelsea took his hand in hers and squeezed.

"When are you going to get it through that thick head of yours?" she said. "We're *all* in this, Quinn. For better or worse."

Ulysses raised an eyebrow. "Did y'all just get married there?"

They ignored him and went over the plan, such as it was. Five minutes later, Ulysses, Bishop and Schuster were back in their helmets, marching the others toward the hangar, and their destiny.

28

"Okay, what the hell?"

Bishop's voice was low over the helmet radio to keep from being picked up by any audio detectors as they reached the entrance to the hangar. They hadn't seen another soul since they left the room where they'd been dropped.

Quinn took Schuster's rifle without a word as they entered the hangar. Both knew that Quinn was the better sniper, which meant he should have the weapon, and that Schuster should be free to work the controls of the ship if they got the opportunity. And now that they'd made it this far without being seen, there was no point in keeping up the disguises.

"Are we finally getting some luck?" Chelsea whispered. "I mean, no one has come for us yet, as far as we know. If they had and found us missing, there'd probably be alarms going off, right?"

Maggott shrugged his massive shoulders. "There's still plenty o'time. Gloom and Ben are wanderin' hither and yon lookin' fer a terminal. If we don't trip an alarm, m'sure they will."

She slapped his arm. "Thanks for the pep talk, Percival."

He snarled at her but kept his mouth shut.

Quinn couldn't believe their luck, which meant that he didn't.

There was no way they had just been left to their own devices in this place; something was wrong. But until they figured out what, they had no choice but to go through with the plan and get on board FUBAR.

He waved them toward the ship, which sat facing out through the open door onto the San Francisco Bay. Quinn felt the ocean breeze on his face as they got closer and marvelled at the sweetness of the air. He'd never known such a clean scent outside of an enclosed, artificially ventilated building before.

The rear door was down, and Schuster led them around to the access port that would get him into the data storage unit. The others hunkered down on the hangar floor to set up reconnaissance points while he worked.

Schuster entered a numeric code that opened a hatch on the outside of the ship and called up the display screen. Quinn watched as a series of numbers ran along the screen, each one followed by a code.

"This isn't right," said Schuster, frowning.

"What's up?" asked Quinn.

He pointed to the scrolling numbers. "These are data files, each with a separate number. But the code that follows is the same for all of them."

"What does that mean?"

"It means that the files were all intact, even after that EMP hit us in space."

"That's great news, isn't it?"

Quinn wanted to get his hopes up, but the look on Schuster's face wasn't encouraging.

"Each one should have its own code, because each file has a separate file size, length, type, a bunch of other data that sets them apart. But these codes are all the same, which means every file is exactly the same."

Quinn felt his heart kick against the inside of his ribs as he heard a voice from inside of FUBAR: "Let me save you the trouble of trying to grasp what he's saying. The files all have the same code because they all have the same content, which is to say no content at all. They've been erased."

Bishop, Ulysses and Quinn were already on the move, surrounding the cargo hold door of the ship and dropping to one knee in a firing pose.

"Come out with your hands up!" Quinn shouted.

"Please don't be so obtuse," said the voice, only now it was behind them.

Quinn and the others spun to face the entrance to see Zero and a tall, thin man with sallow skin and thick glasses. Quinn drew a bead on the man's left thigh and squeezed the trigger of his rifle, preparing himself for the recoil as he slowly let out his breath.

Nothing happened.

Beside him, Bishop and Ulysses were trying to fire their own weapons, with no success. Quinn looked up to see Zero shaking his head.

"You didn't honestly think there were no cameras in that room with you, did you?" he asked. "Please, Quinn, tell me you're not that stupid."

His heart tumbled. They had, indeed, been that stupid. Or maybe just so desperate that they didn't want to let themselves think about it.

"I can control all the weapons and the suits from my own implants," Zero continued. "The guns don't fire unless I want them to. Hell, the suits don't do anything unless I want them to, either."

Pain exploded in Quinn's left ear as an armored fist connected with the side of his head. When he recovered his wits, he turned to see Geordie Bishop goggling at his hand.

"Lee, it wasn't me!" he cried.

"Indeed it wasn't," said Zero. "It was me. The servos in these suits really are marvels of technology. They can read the movements of the human skeletomuscular system and enhance their strength. But they can also be used to move that same system involuntarily. It allows for soldiers to sleep in their suits and still march at the same time, for example, or to perform complex tasks that have been programmed into it. Or, in this case, for me to punch you from way over here."

"Must we?" The other man, whom Quinn assumed was Toomey, sounded impatient. "I need to find out what they know, not play with them as a cat would a mouse. I already wasted enough time erasing those files after I loaded the supplies."

"What are you talking about?" Quinn yelled. "You've obviously been on the ship already! What more do you need from us?"

"And why erase the files?" asked Schuster. "What difference did they make to you?"

Toomey and Zero began walking toward them. Quinn saw Maggott's fists bunch, then immediately go slack again as he saw Zero's hands emerge from behind his back with two huge, ugly pistols in them.

"Dev Schuster, isn't it?" Toomey asked.

Schuster frowned. "Yeah. Dr. Toomey, I presume?"

"I was told that you were less stupid than the others in your group," said Toomey, ignoring the question. "Apparently that appraisal was wrong, otherwise you would know exactly why I erased those files."

"Wait a minute," said Schuster, snapping his fingers. "You didn't want a record of our escape from Oberon, or anything else that happened there, did you?"

"If the information contained in those files had gotten into the wrong hands, it could have caused untold problems."

"You don't get it," said Quinn. "The information in those files is far more important than the tech upgrades on the ship! Those files told the story of what happened on Oberon One! How the aliens took over the minds of the people on the station!"

Toomey sighed. "I watched them, Mr. Quinn. I don't need a recap."

Quinn saw surprise dawn on Zero's face, which told him that Toomey hadn't shared everything with his right-hand man.

"Wait a minute," said Zero. "Are you telling me that Quinn's story was true?"

"There is an alien intelligence on Oberon One, yes," said Toomey. For the first time, Quinn heard inflection in the man's voice. "It is a type of hive mind that has access to the collective knowledge of thousands of species, and it has the use of a heretofore unknown element that allows for quantum leaps in technology."

"Jesus," said Zero. "I don't know what to think about this."

"You don't need to think, Zero. I'll take care of that for us. Once these people have answered my questions, you can dispose of them."

"What questions?" asked Chelsea. "Do they have anything to do with my father?"

Toomey gave her a disdainful frown. "Your father is no longer of any concern to me. I don't need his monetary reward for your return. Not when I have access to this ship."

Quinn felt dread beginning to tickle around the edges of his gut. Toomey had the ship, and the ship could get him back to Oberon One.

"Who have you told your story to?" Toomey asked. "How many other people know what happened on that station?"

At that moment, Quinn saw something behind Toomey and Zero, a quick flash that was over so fast he almost thought he'd imagined it.

Almost. And it was enough to give him a desperate idea.

"Our story?" he said. "What story is that, Toomey? Are you talking about how you kidnapped Frank King in Kazakhstan and framed me and my men for the crime?"

"I asked you not to be obtuse," Toomey sighed. "That had nothing to do with Oberon One. It was simply a means of removing King from the political chessboard to advance the interests of others. I needed to money to fund projects at Prometheus."

Quinn nodded. "Just making sure. So you want to know what happened on Oberon One?"

"Yes!" Toomey snipped. "Get to the point! What do you know, and whom have you told?"

"All right, here goes: a cosmic accident unleashed an alien intelligence on the moon Oberon. That intelligence took over the minds of several people on board that prison station, and once it did, the aliens started building technology that will ultimately open a wormhole to another solar system, which will allow for faster-than-light travel."

"Yes, yes, I know all this," Toomey said tersely.

Schuster frowned. "Wait a minute, you *know* this? How could you possibly, unless... you've been talking to Kergan!"

"Kergan?" Zero seemed confused. "Wait, who the hell is Kergan?"

"Kergan is the host of the alien who took over Oberon One," said Quinn. "He's killed dozens of people, and he's the one overseeing the building of the wormhole."

"Officer Kergan is the most extraordinary intelligence I have ever encountered," said Toomey. The reverence in his voice turned Quinn's stomach. "He has opened my mind to countless possibilities and opportunities I had never imagined before."

Zero stopped walking and grabbed Toomey by the shoulder, prompting the doctor to flinch violently.

"Unhand me!"

"Hold on one goddamn second," said Zero. "I need to get this straight. You two are saying that this is all true? That there's some alien intelligence that wants to take over our minds?"

Toomey shook his head vigorously. "Not take over!" he cried. "Share their knowledge! Bestow their advanced technology upon us!"

"Bring a fookin' army through that wormhole!" Maggott bellowed. "We were there! We know!"

"Officer Kergan has assured me—"

"Kergan is insane," said Chelsea. "You can't trust anything that comes out of his mouth!"

"He's already given us a gift," said Toomey, pointing to FUBAR. "This incredible ship that traversed almost three billion kilometers in only three weeks! Capable of bending light! God alone knows what else it can do."

"God and the ghost of Kevin Sloane," Schuster muttered.

Zero was still clutching Toomey's arm. "This is insane, Toomey."

"It's the next step in human evolution, man!" Toomey's beady eyes were dancing now. "We will be able to move humanity forward a hundred generations in one fell swoop!"

"We'll be giving up our minds to do it!" Quinn cried.

Toomey pulled away from Zero's grasp and smoothed out his white jacket. His eyes were less wild now as he tried to compose himself, but when he spoke, it was with the same dismissive tone.

"None of this matters," he said. "I'm taking the ship to Uranus."

"Like fuck you are," said Zero, his eyes wide. "You think I'm going to let you—"

"Hey Doc, would you mind saying that last line again?" called a voice from the hangar entrance. "Only this time, can you look into the camera?"

Toomey and Zero spun to face the doorway. Quinn grinned as Gloom and Ben stepped out from where he'd spotted them hiding a few minutes earlier.

"What—" Toomey sputtered.

Ben held up a wrist band that looked almost as sophisticated as the one that was part of Zero's smart suit.

"Great camera in these things," he said. "Direct live broadcast capability in full 360."

Gloom grinned. "Streamed live as you were speaking, too, thanks to a little back door action on your servers. You've got some serious network clearance here, I must say. I could get into just about anywhere from these computers."

29

Quinn saw Toomey's mouth drop open two inches as he finally understood what had happened.

"You," he breathed. "You were—"

Ben turned the camera on his wrist toward himself and fixed it with a grim look.

"Friends, it may not seem like it right now, but what you've just witnessed is one of the turning points in human history," he said. "The former head of the Prometheus black site in Antarctica has just admitted that he has been in contact with a hostile alien intelligence that is aboard a SkyLode mining station and prison orbiting Oberon, a moon of Uranus."

"Shut that off!" There was naked panic in Toomey's voice now, and Quinn was encouraged to see Zero grab the man again and hold him in place.

"This revelation will have long-reaching consequences," Ben continued. "But the urgency is real. Humanity must acknowledge this threat, and we must do so immediately. The very fate of humanity hangs in the balance." He turned the camera back toward Toomey. "And this man has proved to us that we cannot trust our government to address it for us. We must hold them accountable, we must take action and we must mobilize, because we may have far less time than any of us can imagine. This is Foster Kenya, and I urge you to stay tuned for updates. The fate of the world may well depend on it."

Gloom rolled her eyes. "A little overdramatic, don't you think?"

"Gotta go with what sells," Ben said with a wide grin.

Quinn felt his own smile widen, knowing that they had finally done what they'd come to Earth to do. No matter what happened from here on, they had accomplished that much.

Chelsea gripped his hand again. "Am I dreaming? Did we do it?"

"Technically, they did it," he said, pointing to Gloom and Ben. "But yeah. Yeah, we did."

Zero's face betrayed his struggle to take in everything that had just happened, but it didn't take long before his confusion turned to anger.

"You're Foster Kenya?" He glowered. "Jesus Christ, you just outed me to the world." He turned to Toomey. "And you! If I'm going down, you're going to break my fall, you ugly little bastard."

"It's over, Zero!" said Quinn. "None of your secrets matter anymore! We need to focus on the aliens!"

"It's over when I *say* it's over!" Zero snarled. He moved to tighten his grip on Toomey's arm and then suddenly froze.

"What the hell...?"

Zero's right hand opened and released Toomey's arm, which revealed a wristband that the doctor had been manipulating beneath his sleeve. Toomey smoothed his sleeve and cleared his throat.

"I can't move!" Zero barked.

"Of course not," Toomey said evenly. "You didn't honestly think I would create smart suits that I couldn't control, did you?"

Quinn turned to see Ulysses, Bishop and Schuster all frozen in place.

"Well, fuck a duck," Ulysses growled.

Toomey began to trot toward FUBAR now, and Quinn moved to intercept him. Maggott flanked him as Gloom and Ben closed the gap from their place in the entrance. It was a classic pincer move that would trap him long before he got to the ship.

Or so Quinn thought.

"Oh, for the love of God," Toomey muttered as he caught sight of his pursuers. He raised his wristband and manipulated the controls, and the next instant, Quinn saw the floor rushing up to meet him.

He landed flat on his nose and came to rest on his side, where he saw the others dropping like flies as well. Maggott was on all fours, trying to crawl to FUBAR, but he didn't make it ten feet before collapsing. Beside him, Chelsea was trying to speak, but all that came out was babble.

Quinn caught movement in the corner of his eye and looked up to see Toomey staring down at him with his little rat eyes.

"The science of infrasonics has saved countless lives," he said. "It can be used to incapacitate without causing permanent harm. Imagine what other amazing discoveries await us, Mr. Quinn. I want you to think about that before you decide on what you do next."

With that, he continued through the cargo hold door and into FUBAR's bridge. As the hatch closed behind him, Quinn thought he saw a grin spreading across Toomey's face.

Seconds later, the engines had ignited and were lifting the ship off the hangar floor and out over the bay. Quinn and the others lay helpless on the floor, dealing with the fading effects of the infrasonic weapon on their brains, as it climbed into the clear, cobalt-blue sky and eventually disappeared.

Slowly, they came back to themselves, and Quinn managed to crawl up onto his ass. He felt like a toddler that had just done a shot of tequila, but he could think again. He shuffled over to Bishop, whose arms had started moving again.

"You... move?" Quinn mumbled.

Bishop nodded. Beside him, Ulysses and Schuster were regaining mobility as well.

"The range," Zero said from ten meters away, where he'd fallen to the floor. He was struggling to get to his feet. "The range... is limited. Once ship... flew... lost control of... suits."

Everyone spent the next several minutes breathing deeply and trying to keep the contents of their stomachs in their stomachs.

Bishop and Ellie were on the floor, hands entwined, while Gloom sat with her head in her hands, moaning.

When Quinn had finally worked up the energy to speak, he crawled over to Ben, who was lying on his side in the fetal position.

"Ben," he croaked. "That was fucking brilliant."

"Doesn't feel brilliant," Ben groaned. "But I appreciate it. This is kind of like having the hangover without having the party first."

"S'okay," Gloom breathed. "No need to thank the one who... got the content out to the audience... with her hacking skills. Just thank the... talking head."

Quinn chuckled softly in spite of his spinning head and churning stomach. He would have to make a note to get to know these two people better now that they all had two minutes to catch their breath.

Then motion caught his attention and he turned to see Zero staggering toward the entrance to the hangar. His suit was obviously helping him move, though it was possible his cyborg physiology was pitching in, too. Quinn had to admit, despite everything else about the man, Toomey's inventions were amazing, and Zero was no exception.

"What will you do now?" he asked, his voice still weak.

Zero frowned. "I don't know. You've had a few weeks to get used to this alien thing, but it's brand new to me. I need time to think."

"Don't take too long," said Chelsea. "There's no time to waste. This shit is real, and it's coming faster than we can imagine."

Zero paused for a moment, then turned to them and nodded.

"I'll say this much: good luck. We're all going to need it."

With that, Zero walked out of the hangar.

"All we been through," Maggott growled. "Ev'rythin' he did to us, an' he just walks away. Dinnae seem right."

"I don't think we have the luxury of being right anymore," said Quinn. "For now, I'll settle for just being alive and not having an alien running around in my head." He turned to Schuster. "No offense, Dev."

Schuster barked a laugh. "Speaking of that, I better figure out how to get in touch with that part of my brain, seeing as how that creepy bastard just stole our ship."

"Hey, I just had an idea," said Bishop.

Ellie snickered. "I thought I smelled smoke."

He gave her a playful poke. "Maybe we can get the reward from Chelsea's father and buy ourselves a new ship."

"Shit," Chelsea muttered. "I forgot about my father. I don't even know if he's on his way here or what."

"Tell you what," said Quinn. "How about we all just lie here until someone finds us?"

"I dunno 'bout that," Ulysses groaned. He was on his back with his knees bent, like he was trying to do sit-ups and failing miserably. "With our luck, it'll be the space cops."

As it turned out, it wasn't space cops who finally showed up. About twenty minutes later, the hangar was awash in men and women wearing fatigues and carrying weapons. They stormed in through the hangar entrance and swept the area. Quinn and the others simply lay there, watching it. They were too exhausted at that moment to care what happened next.

"Clear!"

"Clear!"

"Of course it's clear!" Quinn grumbled. "We did all the fucking work a half-hour ago! Who the hell *are* you, anyway?"

A blond woman with lieutenant bars on her shoulder crouched next to him on the floor, her hand close to her sidearm.

"Napoleon Quinn?" she asked.

"Only if you're not a bill collector."

She nodded to some others who were standing around her and they trotted off to the entrance. About thirty seconds later, they returned, flanking a man in a dark suit. Quinn looked up at the man when he was about ten meters away, wondering absently who he was about to have the honor of meeting. As long as it wasn't a cyborg with his face, he figured he was ahead of the game.

Then he got a good look at the face and realized it belonged not to him, but to someone he had known for quite some time. Around him, the other Jarheads were starting to stare at the newcomer.

"Well, well, well," Quinn drawled. "Fancy meeting you here."

The old man hunkered down on creaking knees so that Quinn could see his face up close. It had been over two years, and he'd lost some more hair in that time, but there was no mistaking those piercing eyes, that hawk nose, the air of command about him.

"It's good to see you again, Captain," said Tribune Morley Drake. "It would seem we have a lot to talk about."

EPILOGUE

Dr. Toomey had never been in deep space before, and he wasn't prepared.

He'd been to orbit many times, of course, but never for weeks at a time. His natural curiosity had been keen for the first several days, but once he reached the asteroid belt, he'd become almost claustrophobic, even though the Raft was far from confining, especially for a lone person.

Luckily, he had Officer Kergan to talk to.

"Tell me again what you did right before you left," his new friend said during their daily holographic commlink call.

Toomey noticed that Kergan had taken to not shaving, and was sporting the beginnings of a passable beard. Toomey himself had never grown so much as a single whisker in all his sixty-four years.

"I activated an infrasonic wave," he said. It was the fourth time he'd told the story, but Kergan didn't seem to tire of it.

"And it knocked them on their asses!" Kergan hooted. "Even your cyborg, Zero!"

"Indeed," said Toomey.

"You're like me. You don't like Quinn or his friends."

"No." Truth be told, Toomey didn't really like anyone, Kergan included. But he liked one thing about their relationship very much.

"May I… see it again?" he asked.

Kergan grinned. "Only if you ask nicely."

Toomey swallowed hard. "Pretty please. With sugar on top."

Giggling, Kergan bent out of the range of the camera for a moment and returned with the hunk of glowing metal. Toomey gazed at it lovingly, as he always did. The very potential of it seemed to sing to him like a siren, telling him of the many great things they would do when they were finally together.

Kergan was less enamored of it, and so enjoyed interrupting Toomey's reverie and chatting. But Toomey supposed there wasn't anything he could do about that.

"I was thinking," said Kergan. "We really should name this element."

"Does it not have a name in your native language?"

"We're sentient thought, Doctor. We don't have a spoken language."

Toomey thought about that for a moment. He supposed that made sense.

"Perhaps we should name it after the moon where it was discovered," he said. "Oberonium. It only makes sense, after all. There's an element named after Titania, the fairy queen and the neighboring moon, so logically, the fairy king should have his own as well."

Kergan frowned. "I guess. I was just thinking of calling it Toomium, after you."

"Yes," Toomey said instantly, his eyes dancing. "Your idea is better. Toomium it is."

"Perfect!" Kergan grinned and clapped his hands together. "Oh, Doctor, we are going to have so much fun when you get here. I just can't wait."

Toomey found himself feeling the same way. Only two more weeks, give or take.

"What should we work on first?" he asked. "The wormhole generator?"

"I've been giving that some thought, as well. I think maybe that needs to take a back seat for the first little while."

"Oh?" Toomey blinked. "Why is that?"

"Just timing. There's something that has to take precedence, I think."

"Over the wormhole? But what?"

Kergan leaned toward the camera and lowered his voice to a conspiratorial whisper.

"Well, Doctor, just between you and me, I don't think we can trust those people you left behind on Earth. Not after they did what you were telling me about, broadcasting our little secret everywhere."

Toomey shook his head. "No one will believe it, I'm quite certain."

"I'm afraid I don't share your optimism, Doctor. I think they *will* believe it, and when they do, they're going to start thinking about coming out here and breaking up our fun." He grinned. "I call it pissing in your corn flakes. Isn't that funny?"

"Yes," said Toomey, forcing himself to smile. "So if not a wormhole, then what *should* be our first project?"

"Well, you know how your infrasonic weapon works? By producing psychedelic effects?"

"Of course."

Kergan's grin widened, until it actually became uncomfortable to look at it.

"I have something that works a little bit like that," he said. "It makes unpleasant images in people's minds. And I'd really like to see just how much stronger we can make it. Because when those people *do* show up, we'll have to stop them. But we don't want to hurt them physically, do we?"

"No," said Toomey. "No, of course not."

Kergan nodded. "I can't wait for you to get here, Doctor."

"Neither can I," said Toomey.

It would be a long time before he finally fell asleep that night in his zero-gravity bed pouch, and when he did, he dreamed of bloody battlefields under alien suns.

THE END